The Princess Play Collection

By

L. Henry Dowell

BLACK BOX THEATRE PUBLISHING

Copyright© 2015 by L. Henry Dowell
ALL RIGHTS RESERVED
CAUTION:
Professionals and amateurs are hereby warned that
THE PRINCESS PLAY COLLECTION
is subject to a royalty. It is fully protected under the copyright laws of the United States of America, the British Commonwealth, including Canada, and all other countries of the Copyright Union. All rights, including professional, amateur, motion picture, recitation, lecturing, public reading, radio broadcasting, television and the rights of translation into foreign languages are strictly reserved. The right to photocopy scripts or videotape performances can be granted only by the author. In some cases, the author may choose to allow this, provided permission has been requested prior to the production. No alterations, deletions or substitutions may be made without the written permission of the author.
L. HENRY DOWELL
All publicity material must contain the author's name, as the sole author of the work.

By producing this play you give the author and
BLACK BOX THEATRE PUBLISHING
the right to use any publicity material including pictures, programs and posters generated from the production.

To order additional copies of the script, or to request performance rights, please contact us at
wwwblackboxtheatrepublishing.com

ISBN 978-0692480830

Printed in the United States of America.

Cover art by John Ridley

Table of Contents

The Odd Princesses	p. 5
Snow White and the Seven Dwarves of the Old Republic	p. 54
Cinderella and the Quest for the Crystal Pump (Small cast)	p. 93
The Little Mermaid (More or Less)	p. 142
Sleeping Beauty in the 25th Century	p. 174
Snow White and the 47 Dwarves	p. 207
Cinderella and the Quest for the Crystal Pump	p. 263
Rapunzel: Escape from Zombie Tower	p. 333

THE ODD PRINCESSES

A Play by L. Henry Dowell

BLACK BOX THEATRE PUBLISHING

CAST
Snow White
Cinderella
Sleeping Beauty
Princess Belle
The Little Mermaid
Rapunzel
Prince Charming
The Other Prince Charming

Additional actors may be used in the party scene to expand the cast. It is recommended that you include traditional princes as dates for Sleeping Beauty, Princess Belle, Rapunzel and The Little Mermaid.

Music choices for the play are entirely the responsibility of the director.

Dedicated to
MaKenzie and Lindsay

THE ODD PRINCESSES
SCENE ONE

MUSIC: Fun intro music plays.

LIGHTS: Rise on a palace. It is a mess with clothes and boxes piled about. A sofa sits at center stage with dresses thrown over the back. A mirror upstage has a sign that reads, "Out of Order". SLEEPING BEAUTY, PRINCESS BELLE, THE LITTLE MERMAID and RAPUNZEL are seated at a table downstage right, playing cards. There are two empty chairs around the table.

PRINCESS BELLE
Hey Rapunzel, you got any sixes?

RAPUNZEL
Yes.

RAPUNZEL hands card to PRINCESS BELLE.

PRINCESS BELLE
What about you, Sleeping Beauty?

SLEEPING BEAUTY has nodded off.

RAPUNZEL
I think she's nodded off…again.

PRINCESS BELLE
(Elbowing SLEEPING BEAUTY.)
Wake up, Sleeping Beauty!

SLEEPING BEAUTY
(Startled.)
What? I didn't do it! I don't know how that got there, officer!

The OTHERS laugh.

SLEEPING BEAUTY
Wait…what's going on? What happened?

RAPUNZEL
You fell asleep again.

SLEEPING BEAUTY
Awww, shoot. I just can't help it.
(Yawning.)
I'm so tired.

RAPUNZEL
You should see someone about your narcolepsy.

THE LITTLE MERMAID
And about your sleeping problem, while you're at it.

The OTHERS shoot HER a look.

SLEEPING BEAUTY
Did I miss anything important?

PRINCESS BELLE
Sixes.

SLEEPING BEAUTY
What?

PRINCESS BELLE
Sixes, dear. Do you have any?

SLEEPING BEAUTY
Oh!
(Looks at HER cards.)
Yes.

Pause.

PRINCESS BELLE
May I have them?

SLEEPING BEAUTY
Oh… yes, of course.

SHE hands PRINCESS BELLE a card.

PRINCESS BELLE
And what about you, Little Mermaid? Do you have any sixes?

THE LITTLE MERMAID
Sixes? Hmmm… Let me see. No, I don't seem to…wait…is that a…no…I guess not. I don't have any sixes…and you know what that means! GO FISH! Bwah-ha-ha-ha-ha!

SHE laughs as the OTHERS just roll THEIR eyes at HER.

RAPUNZEL
Does she have to do that every time?

PRINCESS BELLE
I told you we should play something besides Go Fish.

SLEEPING BEAUTY
It was her turn to pick.

RAPUNZEL
Where's Snow White? I thought she was going to the kitchen to whip us up some sandwiches.

THE LITTLE MERMAID
That's assuming she can find the kitchen. This is Snow White we're talking about here.

THEY laugh.

PRINCESS BELLE
(Yelling towards kitchen.)
Snow White? What's taking so long? We're starving to death out here!

SNOW WHITE
(From offstage.)
Keep your bodices on! I'm working on it!

SOUND: Crashing sounds. Pause.

SNOW WHITE

Oops.

THEY laugh.

RAPUNZEL
You know who makes good sandwiches? Cinderella.

PRINCESS BELLE
She really does. And she takes so much time to make sure they look good too.

THE LITTLE MERMAID
She cuts the crust off the bread and then cuts them into little triangles. I wish she were here.

RAPUNZEL

I agree.

PRINCESS BELLE
What about you Sleeping Beauty?

SLEEPING BEAUTY has nodded off, again.

PRINCESS BELLE
(Elbowing HER, again.)
Sleeping Beauty!

SLEEPING BEAUTY
(Startled, again.)
We're just friends, I swear!

> THEY laugh at HER, again. SNOW WHITE enters, carrying a tray of sandwiches and a tea kettle and cups.

SNOW WHITE
Tea is served, girls!

ALL
Yay!

> THEY EACH take a sandwich and bite into them at the same time. The looks on THEIR faces say it all.

ALL
Yuck!

PRINCESS BELLE
Snow White, these sandwiches are dreadful!

RAPUNZEL
Yes, what did you put in these?

SNOW WHITE
It's my own recipe. The seven dwarves used to love it when I made this. It's peanut butter, cucumber, chili peppers and tuna fish.

THE LITTLE MERMAID
Did you…did you just say…tuna fish??? Oh no! I'm a… I'm a…CANNIBAL!!! A fish that eats other fish…like a shark! I'M A SHARK!!!

> SHE starts bawling.

RAPUNZEL
(Comforting HER.)
There, there, Little Mermaid. You are not a shark.
(SHE shoots SNOW WHITE a dirty look.)
What were you thinking, Snow White?

SNOW WHITE
Sorry…listen, I know what'll make you feel better, Little Mermaid. How about a spot of tea?

PRINCESS BELLE
That's a good idea, let's all have some tea.

> SNOW WHITE fills all of THEIR cups, having to wake SLEEPING BEAUTY, WHO has fallen asleep, and THEY drink at the same time. ALL spit.

PRINCESS BELLE
That tea is atrocious! What did you put in that?

> SNOW WHITE lifts the lid of the teapot and pulls out a long, ugly, wet sock. ALL are grossed out.

SNOW WHITE
I've been looking all over for that sock.

RAPUNZEL
I really miss Cinderella's cooking!

THE LITTLE MERMAID
Me too. She never made me eat…my relatives!

> SHE starts bawling again.

SLEEPING BEAUTY
How can you be such a terrible cook…and house keeper?

SNOW WHITE
I guess the dwarves just weren't that demanding. They thought my cooking and cleaning skills were great and I guess compared to theirs, they were. Look girls, I miss Cinderella's cooking too but she's been much too busy cleaning up after her stepmother and stepsisters to attend our little get-togethers. I hear they treat her like some sort of maid.

PRINCESS BELLE
Speaking of maids, have you thought about hiring one yourself?

SNOW WHITE
You're right. Things have really started piling up since my own stepmother, the Evil Queen left town.

RAPUNZEL
Didn't you used to have a palace full of servants?

SNOW WHITE
My stepmother was so evil she ran them all off before she left.

PRINCESS BELLE
That explains this place.

SNOW WHITE
Look, if you don't like the sandwiches, I'll just order us a pizza. What do you say, girls? Pepperoni, extra cheese, green olives, maybe some anchovies?

> Pause. ALL look at THE LITTLE MERMAID.

THE LITTLE MERMAID
ANCHOVIES???

> SHE starts bawling, again. THEY cross to

comfort HER. SOUND: Doorbell rings.

THE LITTLE MERMAID
(Between bawls.)
Is that it? The anchovy pizza?

SNOW WHITE
Of course not. I haven't ordered it yet.

SOUND: Doorbell rings, again.

SNOW WHITE
I'm coming. I'm coming. Where are the servants in this place, anyway? Oh yeah, I don't have any.

SNOW WHITE exits then re-enters with CINDERELLA, who carries a suitcase.

SNOW WHITE
Look who was at the door, girls.

ALL
Cinderella!

CINDERELLA
Hello, everybody.

SNOW WHITE
We didn't think you were going to make it tonight, Cindy.

CINDERELLA
To be honest, neither did I, Snow White.

THE LITTLE MERMAID
Would you like to sit down? We saved your seat.

CINDERELLA
Thank you, Little Mermaid, that was kind of you but I didn't come to play cards.

PRINCESS BELLE
What do you mean, Cindy?

CINDERELLA
I came because I had no place else to go. You see, I've run away from home.

ALL
What?

SLEEPING BEAUTY
But why, Cinderella?

CINDERELLA
Because I'm tired of being treated like a servant in my own home. "Beat the rugs, Cinderella!" "Milk the cow, Cinderella!" Churn the buttermilk, Cinderella!" Oooh, how I hate buttermilk!

SNOW WHITE
So, you just up and left, huh?

CINDERELLA
Yes, I did…mostly.

PRINCESS BELLE
Mostly? What do you mean, "mostly"?

CINDERELLA
Well…I thought it would be terribly impolite to leave them without anything to eat, so I cooked enough meals to get them through the next week or so. Then I weeded the garden for them and washed all the bed clothes, gathered the eggs, beat the rugs, milked the cow and churned the buttermilk.

SNOW WHITE
I thought you hated buttermilk?

CINDERELLA
Drinking it, yes. Churning it isn't so bad.

RAPUNZEL
And then you left?

CINDERELLA
Yes…well…almost.

PRINCESS BELLE
Almost? What do you mean, "almost"?

CINDERELLA
I had to go back for my friends.

THE LITTLE MERMAID
What friends?

CINDERELLA
These little guys.

> SHE opens suitcase. SOUND: Mice squeaking. The OTHER GIRLS scream and jump up on sofa.

SNOW WHITE
What are you thinking, bringing those rats in here?

CINDERELLA
They aren't rats. They're mice. And they're my friends. In fact, next to you girls, they're the best friends I have in this whole world. I can't tell you how many times they've helped me out when I was in trouble.

SNOW WHITE
Do they have rent money?

CINDERELLA
What?

SNOW WHITE
I was just thinking if they're going to help you out of this situation they're going to need to come up with some rent money. Or maybe they're carpenters? Are they? Maybe they can build you a new house?

PRINCESS BELLE
Stop teasing her, Snow White.

SNOW WHITE
Who's teasing? My fuzzy forest friends were a big help to me with my housework when I stayed with the seven dwarves.

RAPUNZEL
Whatever became of them?

SNOW WHITE
They got tired of working for free. Started demanding that they be paid for their work.

RAPUNZEL
That doesn't seem so unfair, really.

SNOW WHITE
I didn't think so either, at the time. But then they asked for health care and dental, two weeks paid vacation, matching uniforms, unlimited acorn breaks. I finally had to draw the line when they asked for a company expense account. It just seemed extravagant for a bunch of rabbits and squirrels. I had to let the whole crew go.

CINDERELLA
That's so sad.

SNOW WHITE
To be honest, they made more messes than they cleaned up.

CINDERELLA closes the suitcase and sits

it down. The GIRLS step down off the sofa.

PRINCESS BELLE
Don't you have anywhere to stay, Cinderella?

CINDERELLA
Like I said, you girls are my only friends.

THE LITTLE MERMAID
Why couldn't you stay here?

SNOW WHITE
What?

THE LITTLE EMRMAID
There's plenty of space here in the palace, Snow White. The two of you could be roommates! What do you think, girls?

SLEEPING BEAUTY
I think it's a great idea!

RAPUNZEL
I do too!

PRINCESS BELLE
What do you think, Snow?

SNOW WHITE
I don't know. I've lived alone here for long, I'm not sure I'd even be a good roommate.
  (To CINDERELLA.)
What do you think, Cindy? Would you want to be "roomies"?

CINDERELLA
Gosh, Snow...I mean...I wouldn't want to impose or anything.

SNOW WHITE
You wouldn't be imposing, really. I DO have plenty of space here. I doubt we'd even see each other that much.

CINDERELLA
Sure we would! Lots. And we have SO much in common.

SNOW WHITE
We do?

CINDERELLA
Absolutely! We're both young and single!

SNOW WHITE
That's true.

CINDERELLA
We both have terrible stepmothers!

SNOW WHITE
There is that.

CINDERELLA
We both love my cooking!

SNOW WHITE
Well…I am tired of eating my own cooking.

RAPUNZEL
Because you're an awful cook!

SNOW WHITE
My cooking isn't THAT bad.

SLEEPING BEAUTY
Who're you kidding? Your cooking is terrible!

SNOW WHITE
Ok. It's terrible, I admit. Cinderella, if you'd like to do the cooking, fine. You can cook. But that's it. You are my guest and I don't want you lifting a finger to do anything else around here. DO you understand?

CINDERELLA
That sounds great, Snow! We're going to have so much fun together!
>   (Picks up laundry.)

Where does this go?

SNOW WHITE
>   (Takes laundry from HER, throws it back on floor.)

It goes right there. Just leave it where it is.

CINDERELLA
>   (Picking it back up.)

I don't mind, roomie!
>   (SHE picks up boxes.)

Now, what about these?

>   SHE exits with armload of stuff.

SNOW WHITE
>   (Calling to CINDERELLA.)

You don't have to bother with any of that stuff, Cinderella.

>   CINDERELLA enters with vacuum cleaner.

CINDERELLA
It's no bother. I like being helpful.
>   (Turns on vacuum and then turns it off again.)

You know what, Snow White? I think this is the start of a beautiful friendship!

SHE starts the vacuum and begins to sweep
the sofa. The OTHER GIRLS look at
EACH OTHER. LIGHTS: Fade to black.

SCENE TWO

MUSIC: Scene change music fades.

LIGHTS: Rise on the palace, now much cleaner and elegantly decorated. CINDERELLA enters, dusting and then exits on the opposite side of the stage. SNOW WHITE enters, removes HER cape and throws it over the back of the sofa, sits a basket of apples on the table and exits on the opposite side. CINDERELLA enters, sees the cape, picks it up and exits on the opposite side. SNOW WHITE enters with a magazine. SHE sits on the sofa and props HER feet on the coffee table and begins reading the magazine. CINDERELLA enters, sweeping. SHE notices SNOW WHITE'S feet.

CINDERELLA
Snow White, dear?

SNOW WHITE
Yes, Cinderella, dear?

CINDERELLA
Would you mind terribly NOT putting your feet on the table, dear? I just dusted there.

SNOW WHITE
Of course, dear. How thoughtless of me.

CINDERELLA
No problem. I know old habits can be hard to break.

> SNOW WHITE stands and crosses to the table and takes an apple from the basket, takes a bite from it. SHE doesn't like it and puts it back in the basket, taking a different apple. SHE bites into it, and liking it better,

crosses and sits on the sofa. SHE starts to put HER feet on the table again but remembers what CINDERELLA has told HER. SHE begins to read the magazine again. CINDERELLA has been watching. SHE crosses to the table and picks up the apple with the bite taken out.

CINDERELLA
Was there something wrong with this apple?

SNOW WHITE
It was too sour.

CINDERELLA
It's a Granny Smith apple. It's supposed to be sour.

SNOW WHITE
Is that what those are called?

CINDERELLA
Yes.

SNOW WHITE
Well, I don't know who this Granny Smith is but if she's anything like that apple she must be a very sour old lady!

CINDERELLA
If you didn't like it then why did you pick it?

SNOW WHITE
I just thought it was a very pretty apple.

CINDERELLA
You shouldn't waste food.

SNOW WHITE
Oh, pish posh. Give it to your little mice friends.

CINDERELLA
What a good idea. I think I will.

> SHE exits with apple. SNOW WHITE takes a bite of HER apple, then stands and crosses to the table and puts it back in the basket and takes another apple back to the sofa and sits again, reading HER magazine and, forgetting CINDERELLA'S words, props HER feet on the table. CINDERELLA enters.

CINDERELLA
SNOW WHITE!

SNOW WHITE
(Startled.)
WHAT???

CINDERELLA
Your feet!

SNOW WHITE
Oh! Sorry!

> SHE takes them down. CINDERELLA notices the half eaten apple in the basket and crosses to the table.

CINDERELLA
SNOW WHITE!

SNOW WHITE
(Startled, again.)
WHAT???

CINDERELLA
(Holding up apple.)
What was wrong with this apple?

SNOW WHITE
It was too sweet.

CINDERELLA
Too sweet?

SNOW WHITE
Yes. Just like you.

SHE smiles a big broad smile.

CINDERELLA
Snow, do you know what kind of apple this is?

SNOW WHITE
Hey, what do I look like? An apple expert?

CINDERELLA
This is a Red Delicious apple. They're a very sweet apple.

SNOW WHITE
Precisely. It was much too sweet for me.

CINDERELLA
And what about the one you're eating now?

SNOW WHITE
Why, it's just perfect. Absolutely perfect. What do you call this one?

CINDERELLA
A pear.

SNOW WHITE
Oh? I wasn't aware I had picked any pears today.

CINDERELLA
Is that where you've been all day? Picking fruit?

SNOW WHITE
Yes. The girls and I went apple picking at the local orchard. I do wish you could have come along with us. The girls asked what you had been doing.
(Pause.)
By the way, what have you been doing?

CINDERELLA
Cleaning.

SNOW WHITE
That's what I told them. Cindy's been sweeping the floors and beating the rugs and polishing the silverware and dusting the entire palace top to bottom. All 172 rooms of it.

CINDERELLA
173.

SNOW WHITE
173? Really?

CINDERELLA
I should know. I cleaned them all and still had time to cook you a nice dinner.

SNOW WHITE
Is that what that wonderful smell is?

CINDERELLA
That smell is dessert. I made a soufflé.

SNOW WHITE
A soufflé? What is it?

CINDERELLA
Well, a soufflé is a light, fluffy, baked dish made with egg yolks and beaten egg whites combined with various other ingredients and served as a main dish or in this case, sweetened with kumquats and served as a dessert.

SNOW WHITE
Sounds delicious. When's dinner?

CINDERELLA
Thirty minutes ago.

SNOW WHITE
Oh! I'm sorry Cindy. I had no idea you were making dinner.

CINDERELLA
I just assumed you'd be home at a reasonable hour.

SNOW WHITE
What's a reasonable hour?

CINDERELLA
Thirty minutes ago.

SNOW WHITE
Look. I'm sorry. I'm not used to having people wait on me anymore. I appreciate you making this souplay for me.

CINDERELLA
Soufflé. It's French. Soufflé.

SNOW WHITE
I appreciate you making it, however it's pronounced. Since the Evil Queen left I've been playing things by ear around here.

CINDERELLA
(Aside.)
That's obvious.

SNOW WHITE
I eat what I want, when I want. I clean what I want, when I want.

CINDERELLA
(Aside.)
Which is never.

SNOW WHITE
What did you say?

CINDERELLA
Nothing.

SNOW WHITE
Are you upset about something, Cinderella?

SOUND: Doorbell.

SNOW WHITE
Because if you weren't, you're about to be.

CINDERELLA
Who could that be?

SNOW WHITE
What time is it?

CINDERELLA
I think we've already established that it's thirty minutes past...

SNOW WHITE
Yes, yes...thirty minutes past whenever you expected me to be here for dinner. Listen Cindy, I'm very sorry but I forgot to tell you something.

CINDERELLA
Tell me what?

SNOW WHITE
Well...you see...

SOUND: Doorbell.

CINDERELLA
What is it, Snow White? What did you forget to tell me? Who's at that door?

SNOW WHITE
Our dinner guests.

CINDERELLA
DINNER GUESTS? WHAT DINNER GUESTS???

SNOW WHITE
Look. I don't have time to explain. They're two brothers. Princes.

CINDERELLA
PRINCES???

SNOW WHITE
Yes, princes! Two handsome, eligible princes. One of them is named Prince Charming. The other one is…well, I suppose he's the other Prince Charming. They are brothers after all.

SHE crosses to door.

CINDERELLA
Snow White. I am not dressed for dinner guests. Especially not princes. Especially not handsome, eligible princes. I'm wearing my work clothes!

SNOW WHITE
Don't worry. You look fine. You have a nice, domestic look about you.

SHE exits.

CINDERELLA
(To audience.)
Domestic?

SNOW WHITE
(Entering with PRINCES.)
Right this way, gentlemen.

PRINCES enter, handsomely.

SNOW WHITE
Your Highnesses, welcome you to my palace. This is my roommate, Cinderella. Cinderella, this is Prince Charming.

CINDERELLA
(Curtseying.)
Your Highness.

PRINCE CHARMING
(Bowing.)
It is a pleasure, Cinderella.

SNOW WHITE
And this is his brother...the other Prince Charming.

CINDERELLA
(Curtseying.)
Your Other Highness.

THE OTHER PRINCE CHARMING
(Stepping forward, kissing HER hand.)
A distinct pleasure, Cinderella.

PRINCE CHARMING
(Aside.)
Shoot. Why didn't I think of that?

SNOW WHITE
Would you like to sit down, gentlemen?

PRINCE CHARMING
Of course.

HE sits.

THE OTHER PRINCE CHARMING
Ladies first, of course.

PRINCE CHARMING pops back up.

PRINCE CHARMING
Of course. Ladies first.

The GIRLS sit at the ends of the sofa.
PRINCES sit in the middle, wearing swords.
The sofa is crowded.

SNOW WHITE
Are you comfy, gentlemen?

PRINCE CHARMING
Yes, indeed.

THE OTHER PRINCE CHARMING
Quite comfortable, thank you.

CINDERELLA grumbles.

PRINCE CHARMING
(To CINDERELLA.)
Beg pardon?

SNOW WHITE
(Shooting CINDERELLA a dirty look.)
She was just offering to get us some drinks. Weren't you, Cinderella?

CINDERELLA
Drinks? Sure. I'll go get us some drinks.

SHE stands.

SNOW WHITE
Anything special you guys would like? Cinderella is quite domestic.

CINDERELLA
Yep. That's me. "Domestic".

PRINCE CHARMING
I think I'd fancy something exotic. What say you, brother?

THE OTHER PRINCE CHARMING
That sounds lovely, brother. Something exotic for me also!

SNOW WHITE
Make it three then. We'll all have something exotic. Think you can whip up something exotic for us, Cinderella?

CINDERELLA
Exotic. Gotcha.

SHE exits.

SNOW WHITE
Did you have any trouble finding the place?

PRINCE CHARMING
Not at all. Your directions were quite detailed and even if they hadn't been, I'm an excellent tracker.

THE OTHER PRINCE CHARMING
Yes, he's a regular bloodhound. Especially when he's tracking a princess!

PRINCE CHARMING
Oh, you cad!

ALL THREE laugh.

THE OTHER PRINCE CHARMING
Tell me, Snow White, this Cinderella, is she your maid?

SNOW WHITE
Oh no. Not at all. She's my very good friend. She recently left home and needed a place to stay. I suggested she move in here and be my roommate and…well, here we are.

PRINCE CHARMING
That's quite altruistic of you.

SNOW WHITE
Thank you for saying that, Your Highness.

THE OTHER PRINCE CHARMING
She really is quite lovely.

THEY look at HIM.

PRINCE CHARMING
Brother? Are you smitten with Cinderella?

THE OTHER PRINCE CHARMING
I say…I could be…but I only just met her, after all.

PRINCE CHARMING
That's how it happens, brother.

THE OTHER PRINCE CHARMING
How what happens?

PRINCE CHARMING
Love.

THE OTHER PRINCE CHARMING
Love?

SNOW WHITE
Love?

PRINCE CHARMING

Yes, love!
(Stands.)
Love. That which knows neither rank nor class. That which crosses oceans and levels mountains. That which finds us where we are and takes us in its grasp and never releases. It abides no schedule but that of its own keeping. We may search for love the length and breadth of our lives never realizing that it was, after all, right in front of us the entire time.
(SNOW WHITE stands up right in front of HIM.)
Yes...right in front of us...the whole time.

> HE takes SNOW WHITE in HIS arms as if to kiss HER, but CINDERELLA enters with tray.

CINDERELLA

Drinks are served!

> PRINCE CHARMING drops SNOW WHITE on the sofa.

PRINCE CHARMING

Splendid. I'm parched.

THE OTHER PRINCE CHARMING

I'd say! That was a splendid speech, brother.

PRINCE CHARMING

Thank you, brother.

> SNOW WHITE stands up. Obviously upset with CINDERELLA'S timing.
> CINDERELLA passes out drinks.

PRINCE CHARMING

May I offer the toast?

SNOW WHITE
Certainly.

> ALL raise THEIR glasses.

PRINCE CHARMING
To love!

ALL
To love!

> THEY ALL drink at the same time followed by a spit take, except for CINDERELLA who seems to enjoy the drink.

PRINCE CHARMING
This is vile!

THE OTHER PRINCE CHARMING
Yes, what is this hideous concoction?

CINDERELLA
Buttermilk.

ALL
BUTTERMILK???

> THEY start spitting and wiping THEIR tongues on THEIR sleeves. CINDERELLA continues to drink.

PRINCE CHARMING
Help me, brother! I can't get the taste out of my mouth!

THE OTHER PRINCE CHARMING
It's terrible! I've never tasted anything so horrible in the whole of my life! Make it go away!

SNOW WHITE
Cinderella! Why did you serve us buttermilk?

CINDERELLA
You guys said you wanted something exotic. Buttermilk was the most exotic thing we had in the palace.

SNOW WHITE
What about you? You seem to be enjoying it. I thought you hated buttermilk?

CINDERELLA
Not anymore. I seem to have developed a taste for it.

SHE takes a drink of it.

PRINCE CHARMING
Misery!

THE OTHER PRINCE CHARMING
Agony!

BOTH PRINCES
WOE!!!

SNOW WHITE
(To CINDERELLA.)
You're ruining this for both of us!

CINDERELLA
Ruining what?

SNOW WHITE
(To PRINCES.)
I'm so sorry, Your Royal Highnesses! There seems to have been a misunderstanding about the drinks. Hopefully Cinderella's dessert will be more to your liking.

PRINCE CHARMING
Dessert?

THE OTHER PRINCE CHARMING
Did you say dessert?

BOTH PRINCES
WE LOVE DESSERT!

SNOW WHITE
Excellent! Cinderella has been working all day to prepare a soufflé.

PRINCE CHARMING
Oooooo, a soufflé!

THE OTHER PRINCE CHARMING
We love French desserts!

CINDERELLA
(Suddenly.)
Uh oh!
(SHE runs offstage towards kitchen. Pause. From offstage we hear…)
OH NO!!!

> SHE enters carrying the charred remains of the burnt soufflé.

CINDERELLA
(To SNOW WHITE.)
You!

SNOW WHITE
Me?

CINDERELLA
You did this!

SNOW WHITE
What do you mean I did this? It's not my fault you burnt it.

CINDERELLA
Oh, yes it is!

SNOW WHITE
Maybe it's not so bad.

CINDERELLA
It's charred black.

SNOW WHITE
Can we just call it Cajun style?

CINDERELLA
No, we cannot call it Cajun style.

SNOW WHITE
Can't you throw a little whipped cream on it? I'm sure it'll taste fine.

> The TWO of THEM begin to play a cat and mouse game around the sofa. The PRINCES step up on the sofa to avoid THEM.

CINDERELLA
Whipped cream? Whipped cream? Where am I supposed to get whipped cream?

SNOW WHITE
I don't know. The same place you get buttermilk I suppose.

CINDERELLA
You nincompoop!
(PRINCES cover THEIR ears.)
You don't know anything about cooking, do you? You don't put whipped cream on a kumquat soufflé!

SNOW WHITE
Cinderella, let me see it. I'm sure we can figure out something.

CINDERELLA
You want it? Here, you can have it!

> SHE hurls it across the stage, barely missing SNOW WHITE.

BOTH PRINCES
Oh dear!

SNOW WHITE
Calm down, Cinderella. You've gone crazy!

CINDERELLA
Crazy? Crazy? You haven't seen crazy, sister!
   (To PRINCE CHARMING.)
Prince Charming!

BOTH PRINCES
Yes?

CINDERELLA
Give me your sword.

PRINCE CHARMING
Which one of us?

CINDERELLA
It doesn't matter.

THE OTHER PRINCE CHARMING
Mine's sharper!

PRINCE CHARMING
Mine's pointier!

CINDERELLA
Somebody. Give. Me. A. Sword.

THE OTHER PRINCE CHARMING
Here's mine.

> HE hands sword to CINDERELLA. SHE takes it and strikes an attack position.

CINDERELLA
En guard!

SNOW WHITE
All right, Cinderella. I've tried to be nice to you but this time you've pushed me too far. Prince Charming?

BOTH PRINCES
Yes?

SNOW WHITE
That bit's getting old.

BOTH PRINCES
Sorry.

SNOW WHITE
(To PRINCE CHARMING.)
Give me your sword.

> HE hands it to HER. SHE also assumes an attack position.

SNOW WHITE
En guard!

PRINCE CHARMING
I think we'll be going now!

                    THE OTHER PRINCE CHARMING
Yes, thank you very much for a lovely evening!

                    THEY hop off the sofa and run offstage.

                    BOTH PRINCES
MOMMY!!!

                    SNOW WHITE and CINDERELLA lock
                    swords.

                    SNOW WHITE
I hope you're happy, Cinderella. You've run off our dinner guests.

                    CINDERELLA
Maybe if I'd known we were going to have dinner guests in the first place!

                    THEY battle across the palace.

                    SNOW WHITE
Some friend you are! I let you move in here when you had no place else to go!

                    CINDERELLA
Some friend YOU are! You just wanted someone to clean up your messes for you! I am NOT your maid!

                    SNOW WHITE
I told you that you didn't have to clean up anything! But you just can't help yourself! You're some kind of…neat freak!

                    CINDERELLA
Neat freak? Well maybe I am but that's better than being a slob!

                    SNOW WHITE
Slob???

CINDERELLA
Yes, a slob! You are a SLOB, Snow White!

> THEY continue to sword fight until BOTH are tired and collapse on opposite sides of the sofa. Finally, SNOW WHITE stands.

SNOW WHITE
That's it. I've had it. Cinderella, once upon a time we were friends. Because of that and the fact that I know you don't have any other place to go, I'm not going to kick you out. But from now on I want you to stay on that side of the palace and I'll stay on this side. There are 172 rooms here. That should be plenty of space for both of us to live without ever having to see one another. You stay over there. I'll stay over here. You got that?

CINDERELLA
173.

SNOW WHITE
What?

CINDERELLA
There are 173 rooms, remember?

SNOW WHITE
173 rooms. So what?

CINDERELLA
So...who gets the extra room?

SNOW WHITE
Shouldn't I get it? It's my palace.

CINDERELLA
That doesn't quite seem fair.

SNOW WHITE
Fine, Cinderella. Here's what we'll do. We'll divide this room right down the middle. We'll each get exactly half of this room. Does that sound fair?

CINDERELLA
Sure. Except you've got the front door in your half.

SNOW WHITE
There are plenty of doors in this palace. Use the servant's entrance.

CINDERELLA
What did you say?

SNOW WHITE
Uh…look, you've got the kitchen.

CINDERELLA
You didn't even know where the kitchen was until I came here!

SNOW WHITE
Touché.

CINDERELLA
What will you eat?

SNOW WHITE
I'll do what I did before you came along. I'll get take-out.

CINDERELLA
Shall we shake on it then?

SNOW WHITE
Fine.

> THEY meet downstage center and extend THEIR hands. BOTH pause, thinking

better of it. THEY exit on opposite sides. LIGHTS: Blackout.

SCENE THREE

MUSIC: Scene change music plays.

LIGHTS: Rise on palace with a wide white line drawn down the middle of it. The sofa has been removed. SNOW WHITE'S half of the palace is decorated with balloons and a large banner that reads, "B.Y.O.B.". CINDERELLA'S half is decorated a bit more elegant with a pretty banner that reads, "A Night to Remember". Tables are located upstage on each side. SNOW WHITE enters, carrying a stack of pizza boxes. CINDERELLA enters, carrying a pretty cake. EACH sits THEIR food on THEIR table. THEY look at EACH OTHER.
SOUND: Doorbell.

SNOW WHITE
That must be MY guests.

> SHE exits and re-enters with PRINCE CHARMING, PRINCESS BELLE and RAPUNZEL. (NOTE: EXTRAS too, if desired.)

SNOW WHITE
It's so good of all of you to come to my party.

PRINCESS BELLE
(Noticing line.)
Ummmm.....why is there a line drawn down the middle of the palace?

SNOW WHITE
Cinderella and I have decided to live in separate halves of the palace. That's her half and this is mine.

PRINCE CHARMING
Oh, my.

RAPUNZEL
This is silly. She's our friend too. Isn't that right, Cinderella?

CINDERELLA pretends not to hear THEM.

PRINCESS BELLE
Why is she pretending not to hear us?

SNOW WHITE
You'll have to cross the line to talk to her while she's in her side of the room.

THEY look at EACH OTHER.

RAPUNZEL
This is the most ridiculous thing I've ever seen.

SOUND: Knocking.

CINDERELLA
That must be MY guests!

SHE exits and re-enters with THE OTHER PRINCE CHARMING, SLEEPING BEAUTY and THE LITTLE MERMAID. (NOTE: EXTRAS too, if desired.)

CINDERELLA
I'm so glad all of you could make it to my ball.

SLEEPING BEAUTY
We wouldn't have missed it for the world, Cinderella.

THE OTHER PRINCE CHARMING
Yes, but why did we have to enter through the servant's entrance?
(Notices PRINCE CHARMING.)
Oh, hello there brother!

PRINCE CHARMING
Hello to you!

THE OTHER PRINCE CHARMING
I didn't know you'd also been invited to this party.

PRINCE CHARMING
To be quite honest, I'm not sure "that" party is "this" party.

THE LITTLE MERMAID
What's going on here, Cinderella?

CINDERELLA
(To HER GUESTS.)
Snow White and I have divided up the palace.

SNOW WHITE
(To HER GUESTS.)
I decided that I was going to have a party.

CINDERELLA
I wanted to throw a ball.

CINDERELLA and SNOW WHITE
So she decided to copy me!

> The TWO of THEM turn and shoot the OTHER a dirty look.

PRINCESS BELLE
So, you decided to have your parties at the same time?

CINDERELLA and SNOW WHITE
Apparently.

CINDERELLA
Mine is a ball. An elegant ball. See the theme?
(Points to banner.)
"A Night to Remember".

RAPUNZEL
(Pointing to SNOW WHITE'S banner.)
B.Y.O.B.? What does that stand for, Snow White?

SNOW WHITE
What else? Bring your own boyfriend.

> EVERYONE laughs, except
> CINDERELLA.

CINDERELLA
I have prepared wonderful hors d'oeuvres and this beautiful cake.

> HER GUESTS are impressed.

SLEEPING BEAUTY
What are you serving, Snow White?

SNOW WHITE
Pizza and root beer.

CINDERELLA
Maybe we should dance first. That way we can work up our appetites. I've assembled the finest classical musicians in the kingdom to perform for us this evening.

> SHE motions towards the audience/tech
> booth. SOUND: A beautiful waltz plays as
> CINDERELLA and HER GUESTS dance.
> SNOW WHITE interrupts.

SNOW WHITE
(To audience/tech booth.)
Cut that out!
(Music stops.)
You see, I have assembled some of the finest musicians myself, from all over the kingdom to help us get down with our bad selves!
(Motions to audience/tech booth.)
Hit it!

> SOUND: Rock music plays as SNOW WHITE and HER GUESTS dance. THEY are interrupted by CINDERELLA who motions for SNOW WHITE'S band to stop and HER orchestra to resume. This goes on between them until both are playing at the same time. The TWO GROUPS fall over EACH OTHER.

CINDERELLA and SNOW WHITE
CUT!!!

> SOUND: Music stops.

SNOW WHITE
Do you see what you've done? You've ruined my party!

CINDERELLA
You're party? What about my ball?

SNOW WHITE
No one was enjoying your ball, anyway.

THE LITTLE MERMAID
I was enjoying it.

> ALL shoot HER a dirty look.

THE LITTLE MERMAID
Well, I was.

SLEEPING BEAUTY
This is crazy! We're all friends here.

PRINCESS BELLE
That's right! And that includes the two of you! What are you fighting over, anyway?

SNOW WHITE
I don't know...

CINDERELLA
She doesn't appreciate me!

SNOW WHITE
Yes I do, Cinderella!

CINDERELLA
She thinks I'm her maid!

SNOW WHITE
You're wrong. I never wanted you to feel that way. I know all too well what it's like to have to wait on someone hand in foot. My stepmother, the Evil Queen was just...well...evil... and messy. And don't even get me started on the seven dwarves! I may have picked up some bad habits from them, I'm afraid. To be completely truthful and honest with you Cinderella, I thought you enjoyed cleaning. Do you?

CINDERELLA
Well...to be completely truthful and honest, Snow White...no. I don't.

SNOW WHITE
Oh?

CINDERELLA
I hate cleaning. Sweeping the floors. Beating the rugs. Milking the cow.

SNOW WHITE
What about churning the buttermilk?

CINDERELLA
Buttermilk isn't so bad, if you give it a chance.

ALL except CINDERELLA
Yuuuck!

CINDERELLA
What I do like, is to feel needed. And it was obvious that you needed help around here.

SNOW WHITE
Yes, I did. And I still do, if you'll stay. And you don't have to clean anything at all.

CINDERELLA
Let's not get crazy here, Snow.
        (Pause.)
I'll stay…but only if you'll take this ridiculous line down!

ALL look at SNOW WHITE

SNOW WHITE
Done.

THEY hug.

RAPUNZEL
Why don't we make this one big party?

SNOW WHITE
Absolutely! Would you like a piece of pizza, Cinderella?

CINDERELLA
Only if you'll have a piece of my cake, Snow White.

> SNOW WHITE gets pizza. CINDERELLA gets a piece of cake. THEY meet downstage center and as THEY are about to offer it to EACH OTHER, THEY smash it into the OTHER'S face. PAUSE. EVERYONE waits to see what will happen next.

CINDERELLA and SNOW WHITE
BWAH-HA-HA-HA-HA!!!

> EVERYONE laughs. SNOW WHITE looks at audience/tech booth.

SNOW WHITE
Do you think all of you could find something to play together?

> SOUND: Music plays as the CAST dances together. LIGHTS: Fade to black.

THE END

Snow White

and

The Seven Dwarves of the Old Republic

BY

L. HENRY DOWELL

BLACK BOX THEATRE PUBLISHING

CAST

Snow White
The Magic Mirror
The Evil Queen
The Huntsman
Prince
The Seven Dwarves

In the script The Seven Dwarves are numbered #1 - #7. They have purposely NOT been named. At the beginning of the play the audience may be polled in order to name the Dwarves. The actors must then act their parts based on the names that the audience has selected for them. In past productions a list of possible names was chosen through the rehearsal process and printed in the program. Some of those names which were quite effective and funny were:

Stinky	Baby
Moody	Nerdy
Macho	Nose Picker
Itchy	Flirty
Shakespeare	Brainy
Cheerleader	Cowboy
Overactive Bladder	Hillbilly
Director	Gangster
Elvis	Military
Old Geezer	Stevie Wonder
Foreigner	

These names are only suggestions. Feel free to discover other possibilities. The lines remain the same; it's the way they are played which provides the comedy in the Dwarves' scenes. It is advisable to have a selection of props and hats backstage that might be used in connection with the names that are picked by the audience. Casts should be discouraged, however, from improvising lines during the performance. If played by a talented cast, this show has proven to be one that audiences return to for multiple performances.

Above all, the roles in this play should be played with maximum Gusto! Theatre should always be fun!

The action of this play is continuous. When a scene ends on one part of the stage, the lights blackout, but immediately rise on another part of the stage. If your production requires time between scenes, scene change music may be used in addition to the suggested music styles in the play.

SNOW WHITE
AND
THE SEVEN DWARVES OF THE OLD REPUBLIC

Scene: The pre-show lights illuminate the stage. On stage right there is a castle wall with a large mirror hanging from it. The back of the stage contains a forest, and on stage left a small cottage of THE DWARVES with a table and several small chairs. THE SEVEN DWARVES enter and the audience chooses seven names for THEM from a list. This process can be handled by a cast member, or Director. Throughout the play THEY will play THEIR characters based on those names. When THEY exit, the play begins. There is SPOOKY MUSIC. The LIGHTS rise on THE MAGIC MIRROR, whose face now appears in the mirror on the wall.

MIRROR
Good evening everyone. I am the Magic Mirror on the wall, and I'm here to tell you the story of Snow White and the Seven Dwarves. Now first let me assure you that word is pronounced "Dwarves" with a "v" and not "Dwarfs" with an "f" as you may have seen elsewhere.
(Clears throat, comically.)
One snowy night in a castle far, far away, a little princess was born.
(A loud, crying baby is heard.)
Her parents named her Snow White. As the years passed, the child grew up to be a lovely young woman. Her beauty and her gentle nature won the hearts of all who knew her. But of all her attributes, the greatest was her lovely singing voice.

> SNOW WHITE enters in potato sack, singing a Motown tune.

MIRROR
You go girlfriend.

SNOW WHITE
Thank you very much.

MIRROR
No. I mean you go...offstage now.

SNOW WHITE
Oh.

SHE exits.

MIRROR
After Snow White's father died, she lived in the castle with her stepmother, the Evil Queen.

QUEEN enters, dressed in black, and strikes a pose.

MIRROR
As you can see, the Queen was very beautiful, but she was also cold and heartless.

QUEEN
I heard that!

MIRROR
It's true. The mirror doesn't lie. She was also extremely jealous of Snow White's beauty.

QUEEN
I am not!

MIRROR
Are too!

QUEEN
Am not!

MIRROR
Are too!

QUEEN
Am not!

MIRROR
She was also a little childish.

QUEEN
Just get on with it!

MIRROR
Very well…the Queen dressed the Princess in rags and forced her to clean the entire castle like a maid.

> SNOW WHITE enters dressed in a potato sack. SHE carries a bucket and wears rubber gloves. SHE scrubs the floor. SHE works hard and sings "Swing Low, Sweet Chariot"

QUEEN
You missed a spot.

MIRROR
Despite the back breaking work and rough treatment, Snow White never lost her sunny disposition.

SNOW WHITE
I did miss a spot! How nice of you to point that out Evil Stepmother.

> SHE exits.

MIRROR
The Queen's most prized possession was her gorgeous, antique magic mirror…let me tell you, it was beautiful, with a hand carved frame and a…

QUEEN
Ok, ok, we get it.

MIRROR
Every day the Queen would stand in front of her mirror…well, in front of me, and ask a question…

QUEEN
Magic Mirror on the wall, who's the fairest one of all?

MIRROR
And every day, the mirror, who was very articulate, would reply…

"You O' Queen are the fairest in the land."

QUEEN
(To audience.)
Darn tootin!

SHE exits.

MIRROR
While the Queen spent the majority of her time admiring herself, poor little Snow White had to work long hours in the castle, often singing and dancing while she worked.

> DANCE MUSIC begins. SNOW WHITE enters, dancing with a broom. SHE exits and re-enters with a feather duster. SHE exits then re-enters with a toilet plunger. MUSIC ends.

MIRROR
One day, while Snow White was…plunging the toilet, she made a special wish.

SNOW WHITE
Oh how I wish with all my heart that a handsome Prince would come along and carry me away!

MIRROR
No sooner had Snow White uttered those words than a handsome "Prince" appeared!

> PRINCE MUSIC. A purple light illuminates PRINCE. HE wears all purple with high heels. HE dances as the MUSIC blares. HE dances around HER. MUSIC ends.

PRINCE
Hey Baby.

SNOW WHITE
Why, hello there.

PRINCE
You sure are pretty. I dig tall chicks.

SNOW WHITE
Thank you…uh….Prince.

MIRROR
Although Prince was an interesting character, Snow White was very shy.

SNOW WHITE
I'm very shy.

PRINCE
I can dig that.

SNOW WHITE
Have we met before?

PRINCE
I don't think so.

SNOW WHITE
You seem very familiar to me.

PRINCE
Of course I do. I'm Prince, and I brought you a present.

SNOW WHITE
A present! What is it?

PRINCE
Well, a present is a gift you give to someone, but that really isn't important right now. Here.

Hands HER a box. SHE opens it.

SNOW WHITE
Wow….it's a…purple hat.

PRINCE
It's not just a hat. It's a raspberry beret. The kind you find in a second hand store.

SNOW WHITE
Wow. Thanks big spender. I'll treasure it always.
(Throws it into audience.)

MIRROR
Prince was quite smitten with Snow White.

PRINCE
I am quite smitten with you.

MIRROR
Snow White on the other hand wanted to take things a little slower.

SHE starts to say something, but then runs away.

PRINCE
(To audience.)
I love it when they play hard to get.

HE exits.

MIRROR
That evening, as usual, the Evil Queen stood before her Magic Mirror...

QUEEN enters.

QUEEN
Magic Mirror on the wall, who's the fairest one of all?

MIRROR
Well Queen, you see...

QUEEN
Mirror?

MIRROR
It's kind of like this...

QUEEN
Tell me!

MIRROR
Are you sure you really want to know?

QUEEN
Of course I do. Why would I have asked you unless I wanted to know?

MIRROR
You may not like the answer O' Queen!

QUEEN

Really?

MIRROR

Well…

QUEEN
(Extremely mad. Yelling.)
Tell me! I command you!

MIRROR

As you wish.
(Clears throat.)
"Her lips blood red. Her hair like night. Her skin like snow. Her name…Snow White!"

QUEEN
(Flipping her lid.)
SAY WHAT??? How can this be? She's so…cheerful and…
(Looks for another word, but can't think of one.)
Cheerful! Mirror, do you really think she's more beautiful than me?

MIRROR

I calls 'em like I sees 'em.

QUEEN stomps back and forth.

MIRROR

The Evil Queen was so furious she immediately called for her Huntsman.

QUEEN
(Screaming.)
HUNTSMAN!!!!!!!!!

HUNTSMAN enters running. HE is a timid man dressed in grey and green. HE wears a green helmet.

HUNTSMAN
Yes my Queen?

QUEEN
Huntsman. Tomorrow I want you to lead Snow White deep into the Black Forest and kill her!

HUNTSMAN
But why my Queen? She is only a child!

QUEEN
You will do as I command Huntsman, or I will have you thrown into the deepest, darkest pit I can find, and you will stay there for the rest of your miserable existence! Do you understand me, Huntsman?

HUNTSMAN
Yes my Queen. I understand.

> QUEEN exits. THE HUNTSMAN lingers, uneasy, then exits.

MIRROR
Early the next morning, as he had been instructed to do, the Huntsman took Snow White deep into the Black Forest, where he intended to kill her.

> The LIGHTS are low and spooky. SNOW WHITE enters through the forest. SHE is wearing HER Princess costume. THE HUNTSMAN enters behind HER.

SNOW WHITE
Huntsman. Why have you brought me so deep into the Black Forest?

HUNTSMAN
Your evil stepmother…the Queen, thought you might…well, she thought some fresh air might do you well Princess.

SNOW WHITE
But it's so dark here in the forest...I can hardly see my hand in front of my face.
(SHE turns away from the HUNTSMAN.)

MIRROR
The Huntsman knew that if he was going to do it, it would have to be now. He drew his sword.

THE HUNTSMAN draws HIS sword. SNOW WHITE doesn't notice, though the audience will. SHE kneels down and HE raises HIS sword to strike. SHE turns and sees HIM, and is terrified. BOTH freeze.

MIRROR
But he couldn't do it.

HUNTSMAN drops HIS sword and falls to HIS knees.

HUNTSMAN
Please forgive me Princess. The Queen...your Stepmother is horribly jealous of you. She...ordered me to bring you deep into this forest and to...kill you...but I couldn't do it. I could never harm you. I knew your father...he was a very good man...and my friend. But listen to me, you are not safe. You must run even deeper into the forest! Run until you can run no more! And you must never return! Do you understand me Princess?

SNOW WHITE
Yes, I think so.

HUNTSMAN
Run then. I'll tell the Queen the job has been done.

SHE starts off, and then turns to HIM.

SNOW WHITE
Thank you, Huntsman. You really are a good man.

>SHE exits running.

HUNTSMAN
If the Queen learns of what I have done, I will really be a <u>dead</u> man.

>LIGHTS fade on HUNTSMAN.

MIRROR
Snow White was so frightened by what the Huntsman had said that she ran over the hills and across the green until at last she came to a small cottage nestled among the trees.

>LIGHTS rise on Dwarf house. SNOW WHITE enters.

SNOW WHITE
What a charming little house. I wonder if anyone's at home.

>SHE walks through door.

SNOW WHITE
Hello? Is anyone there? My goodness, this place is an awful mess. And everything is so short. I wonder if this house belongs to children.
(A thought occurs to HER.)
Maybe if I tidy up this house a bit, the children who live here will let me stay for a while.

>DANCE MUSIC. SNOW WHITE cleans again. SHE enters with broom, dancing and singing. SHE sweeps, then exits. SHE re-enters with feather duster. SHE dusts, then exits. SHE re- enters with floor buffer, or if that isn't available, the plunger again. MUSIC ends.

SNOW WHITE
(Yawning.)
Gosh. All this house cleaning has made me very tired.
(Pokes HER head in other room.)
Ahhh, how cute. Seven little beds. Maybe whoever lives here won't mind if I take a little nap.

> SHE exits with floor buffer. MUSIC. THE SEVEN DWARVES enter, ALL wearing brown hooded robes, doing a little dance step together and singing. THEY stop outside the cottage, and simultaneously each one does something to indicate what THEIR names are. Then, THEY enter cottage. THEY are muttering and grumbling, and then all stop at the exact same time and look around.

DWARF #1
Great Oogly moogly!

DWARF #2
Someone's been here!

DWARF #3
Someone's cleaned the place up!

DWARF #4
Who would dare?

DWARF #5
Look at them dishes! They're clean!

DWARF #6
Someone did the dishes too?

> DWARF #6 exits to other room.

DWARF #7

Unbelievable!

DWARF #1

My fellow Dwarves...I believe what we have here is one of them ghosts!

DWARF #2

A ghost that does dishes?

DWARF #3

I didn't know ghosts did dishes!

DWARF#4

How can you be so sure?

DWARF #1

Well, I know it wasn't the fuzzy forest creatures running around out there!

DWARF #5

Well of course not. That would be silly.

DWARF #6
(From other room.)

Oh my gosh!

DWARF #7

What is it?

DWARF #6

Someone cleaned the toilet!

> ALL DWARVES rush into other room. A toilet is heard flushing.

DWARVES
(Offstage.)

Oooooooooooooooo!

DWARF #7
(Offstage.)
Who would stoop so low?

DWARF #1
(Offstage.)
Maybe it was that girl sleeping in our bed over there.

> There is a beat.

DWARVES
GIRL!!!!

> DWARVES come running back on in a panic screaming and running into EACH OTHER. SNOW WHITE enters.

SNOW WHITE
Wait a minute! What's wrong?

> DWARVES stop. Beat.

DWARF #2
It's a girl! Run!!!

> DWARVES run around again.

SNOW WHITE
Wait a minute! Wait a minute! Why are you so afraid of a girl?

DWARF #3
Because girl's have cooties!

> DWARVES run around again screaming "Cooties!"

SNOW WHITE
Stop running around and screaming! I can assure you that girls do not have cooties! I do not have cooties!

> DWARVES have settled down. Slowly THEY approach HER.

DWARF #4
Are you sure you don't have cooties?

SNOW WHITE
Certainly not. My name is Snow White. What are your names?

DWARF #1
My name is _____.

> HE uses the name the audience has given HIM, and acts out whatever it implies. Each DWARF steps forward and does the same thing in turn.

SNOW WHITE
Those are very…creative names.

DWARF #1
Don't blame us, we didn't pick 'em.
(Points to audience.)

SNOW WHITE
And do you midgets live here all alone?

> DWARVES look at each other.

DWARF #2
Excuse me?

DWARF #3
I'm sorry. Did she just call us midgets?

DWARF #4
I think she did!

DWARF #5
The nerve!

DWARF #6
We are not midgets!

DWARF #7
We're Dwarves! Don't you know the difference?

SNOW WHITE
Why no…what is the difference?

DWARF #7
Uh…well, we Dwarves…we're better dancers!

DWARVES
Yeah!

> CLASSICAL TYPE MUSIC plays and THEY dance.

SNOW WHITE
Gee. I never knew that about Dwarves.

DWARF #1
I'm sure there's a lot you don't know about Dwarves. And by the way, what are you doing in our house?

DWARVES
Yeah! Tell us! What's going on? What are you doing here? Etc!

> (NOTE: The same DWARF should say "Etc." each time.)

SNOW WHITE
(Beginning to cry.)
Oh…it's so horrible!

DWARF #2
Ah…please don't cry Snow White…you'll make me cry.
(HE does.)

THEY ALL cry. Bawl actually.

DWARF #3
(Crying.)
Why are we all crying?
DWARF #4
(Crying.)
Because it's so darn sad!

SNOW WHITE
But you haven't even heard my story yet.

DWARF #5
(Crying.)
Tell us! Tell us!

THEY gather around HER. ALL blow THEIR noses simultaneously.

SNOW WHITE
Well, my Stepmother is the Evil Queen.

DWARF #6
Ooooh, she's evil!

SNOW WHITE
Yes, we've established that already. Anyway, she tried to have me killed, so I ran away.

DWARF #7
Where'd you run to?

THEY all look at HIM.

DWARF #1

Where do you think she ran away to nincompoop? She ran here.

DWARF #7

Oh yeah. That makes sense.

DWARF #1

Listen, Snow White, if you want to, you can stay with us. We won't let anything happen to you, will we fellas?

DWARVES

You bet! No problem! Sure! Glad to help! Etc.

DWARF #1

We were all great warriors once. In the days of the Old Republic.

DWARVES strike warrior poses.

SNOW WHITE

Oh thank you so very much!

SHE kisses DWARF #1 on the head. The other DWARVES are dumbfounded.

DWARF #2

I hope she doesn't have cooties.

SNOW WHITE

I don't have cooties.

DWARF #1
(Lovey dovey.)
She doesn't have cooties.

DWARF #3

What?

DWARF #1

Nothing.

SNOW WHITE
If you are willing to let me stay here then I insist you let me earn my keep. I'll keep this place clean and I'll cook for you.

DWARVES

Cook?

DWARF #2
You mean real food? Like fried chicken?

DWARF #3

And cornbread?

DWARF #4
And taters? I love me some taters!

DWARVES

Mmmm taters!

SNOW WHITE
And jam cake? Do you like jam cake?

DWARF #5
Ma'am…we adore jam cake.

SNOW WHITE
Then it's settled. Tonight for supper we will have jam cake!

> The DWARVES do a little happy jam cake dance.

SNOW WHITE
Now while I whip up the jam cake it'll give you guys just enough time to wash up.

DWARVES
(To audience.)
WASH UP???

BLACKOUT. Lights rise on MIRROR. QUEEN stands before HIM.

QUEEN
Ok. Let's try this again. Magic Mirror on the wall, who's the fairest one of all?

MIRROR
Uh oh!

QUEEN
Are we going to do this again?

MIRROR
Well, you see…

QUEEN
Just tell me already!

MIRROR
Very well.
(Clears throat.)
"Over the river and across the green, Snow White's still fairer than you my Queen."

QUEEN
SAY WHAT???

MIRROR
You asked.

QUEEN
How can this be?
(Yelling.)
HUNTSMAN!!!!!

HUNTSMAN enters.

HUNTSMAN
Yes, my Queen?

QUEEN
Huntsman. Do you remember that little job I asked you to take care of for me?

HUNTSMAN
(Being coy.)
Which job would that be my Queen?

QUEEN
You know. The one where I asked you to take Snow White deep into the Black Forest and kill her.

HUNTSMAN
Oh...that job.

QUEEN
Yes. That job! Did you do it or not?

HUNTSMAN
(Thinking.)
Yes.

QUEEN
Yes...which?

HUNTSMAN
Not.

QUEEN
Not…what?

HUNTSMAN
Not. You asked if I did it or not. The answer is not.

QUEEN
And why…not…may I ask?

HUNTSMAN
Well…

QUEEN
Never mind. I'm sure the answer would bore me anyway. Do you know the punishment for disobedience…or not?

HUNTSMAN
(Very scared.)
Not?

> SHE raises HER hands in choking motion. HUNTSMAN grabs HIS throat as if HE were choking. HE falls to the ground. BLACKOUT. LIGHTS rise on DWARVES standing around a wash tub looking into it.

DWARF #1
It's so…clean…and bubbly.

DWARF #2
Who's gonna go first?

DWARF #3
Not me. I had my bath already!

DWARF #4
When was that?

                    DWARF #3
Last April.

                    DWARF #5
Somebody has to get in.

                    DWARF #6
Who's it gonna be?

                    DWARF #7
Not me!

                    DWARVES
Not me! Not me! Not me! Etc.

                    DWARF #1
I know. Let's all get in at the same time.

                    THEY all look at HIM.

                    DWARVES
SAY WHAT???

                    DWARF #1
It's the only fair thing to do.

                              ALL shrug, then step in. If the tub is big
                              enough, ALL sit down.

                    DWARF #1
Now see. This isn't so bad.

                    DWARF #2
Shouldn't we have taken our clothes off first?

                    DWARVES
Aaaaaaaaaahhhh.

DWARF #3
Is this one of them whirlpool tubs I've heard so much about?

DWARF #4
I don't think so. Why do you ask?

DWARF #3
I was just wondering where all those bubbles were coming from.

> Beat. Then ALL DWARVES realize someone has farted.

DWARVES
Oooooooooooooohhhh!

> THEY jump out of tub and run away. DWARF #6 stays in tub, looks at audience and just grins. BLACKOUT. LIGHTS rise on QUEEN.

QUEEN
You know, if you want something done right you have to do it yourself.

> In this scene MIRROR keeps sticking HIS tongue out at QUEEN, but stops when SHE turns to look at HIM. SHE holds up a magic potion.

QUEEN
When I drink this magic potion it will transform me into a hideous old hag and Snow White will never be able to recognize me.

> SHE drinks potion. LIGHTS go berserk. There is smoke. QUEEN puts on hag mask and hooded robe. SHE holds a sack.

QUEEN

And now...
>(She reaches in sack and pulls out an apple core.)

Ok...who ate my apple?

> MIRROR has been chewing something but stops. SHE reaches into sack again.

QUEEN

Let's see what else we have in here.
>(Pulls out a kumquat.)

What's this?

MIRROR

That O' Queen, is a kumquat.

QUEEN

A kumquat? What's a kumquat?

MIRROR

A kumquat is a subtropical. pulpy, citrus fruit, used chiefly for preserves.

QUEEN

Really? I never knew that. Well, it'll just have to do.

> SHE pours potion over it and waves HER hands as if casting a spell.

QUEEN

One bite of this poison...kumquat, and Snow White will sleep forever! Bwah-ha-ha-ha-ha!

> BLACKOUT. LIGHTS rise on DWARVES and SNOW WHITE. THE DWARVES are in line to head off to work, each getting a kiss from SNOW WHITE and then exiting. DWARF #1 is last.

DWARF #1

Beware of strangers Snow White. There's no telling what the Evil Queen will do if she finds out that you're still alive.

SNOW WHITE

Don't worry. I'll be careful.

DWARF #1

May the Dwarf be with you!

> DWARF #1 starts off, then comes back for a kiss. SNOW WHITE begins to work. There is a knock at the door.

SNOW WHITE

I wonder who that could be.

> SHE opens door. QUEEN is standing there, in disguise.

QUEEN

Are you here all alone girl?

SNOW WHITE

Why, yes. Who are you?

QUEEN

Just a little old lady happening by. Where are the other people who live here?

SNOW WHITE

They've gone to work for the day.

QUEEN

Excellent. Excellent.

> THE QUEEN walks right past SNOW WHITE into the cottage.

SNOW WHITE
I beg your pardon?

QUEEN
Never mind. And what are you doing this fine morning?

SNOW WHITE
I was just about to bake a pie.

QUEEN
A pie?
(To audience.)
How fortuitous!

SNOW WHITE
(To audience.)
Fortuitous?
(To QUEEN.)
How so?

QUEEN
Well, you see. I just happen to be carrying a basket full of yummy kumquats here and I was wondering if you would like to have some for your pie?

SNOW WHITE
Kumquats? What are kumquats?

QUEEN
Well, they're a subtropical, pulpy, citrus fruit, used chiefly for preserves, but they also make great pies my dear.

SNOW WHITE
You know, I don't think I have ever had a kumquat pie before.

QUEEN
And what's more, these are very special kumquats.

SNOW WHITE
Really?

QUEEN
Absolutely! You see, these are magic wishing kumquats!

SNOW WHITE
Really? Magic wishing kumquats?

QUEEN
Of course. Would I lie?

SNOW WHITE
I have no idea. I just met you.

QUEEN
Oh, I'm very honest. Take my word for it. Would you be interested in making a special wish?

SNOW WHITE
Yes. Yes I would.

QUEEN
Here you go.

>   Hands SNOW WHITE a kumquat.

SNOW WHITE
It's a funny looking little thing isn't it?

QUEEN
Don't judge it by its outside appearance Snow White. You never know what it might be like on the inside...don't forget to make a wish.

>   SNOW WHITE closes HER eyes and makes a wish.

QUEEN
Now take a bite.

SNOW WHITE
Ok.

> SHE bites into it. There is a pause as SHE chews. Then SHE chews some more. Then SHE chews some more. QUEEN looks at HER watch and whispers to HERSELF…

QUEEN
Come on…I don't have all day.

SNOW WHITE
You know…this tastes kind of like…urk!

> SHE falls to the floor.

QUEEN
Now my pretty little Princess, you will sleep forever! Bwah-ha-ha-ha-ha!

> BLACKOUT. LIGHTS rise on MIRROR.

MIRROR
Snow White had fallen into a deep, deep sleep. A sleep so deep that only the kiss of her one true love could awaken her.

> PRINCE MUSIC plays. PRINCE enters.

PRINCE
That's my cue baby.

MIRROR
Hello Prince.

PRINCE
What's shakin' baby?

MIRROR
Oh, not much thank goodness. I wouldn't want to get knocked off the wall.
> (MIRROR laughs waaaaaay too long at HIS joke.)

PRINCE
Yes. Ha ha. That's a good one.

MIRROR
Thanks. So what brings you here?

PRINCE
I'm looking for that cute chick that used to work here....uh, Snow White was her name I think.

MIRROR
Well, Prince. She's over the river and across the green, but she's just been whammied by the Evil Queen.

PRINCE
Bummer.

MIRROR
Luckily, a kiss from her one true love can awaken her from her eternal slumber!

PRINCE
Really? Oh baby! Bring on the smooches!

> PRINCE takes a shot from HIS breath spray, then practices smooching technique.

HUNTSMAN
(Entering.)
Unfortunately, he isn't her one true love.

MIRROR
Huntsman! How did you escape the deep, dark pit?

                    HUNTSMAN
It's a long story and we haven't much time.

                    MIRROR
What were you saying? Prince isn't Snow White's true love?

                    HUNTSMAN
Absolutely not!

                    PRINCE
How can you possibly know that?

> HUNTSMAN whispers in PRINCE'S ear.
> MIRROR struggles to overhear.

                    PRINCE
Oh…gross!!!!!

> PRINCE spits and wipes tongue on arm.

                    MIRROR
Huntsman? Are you certain of this?

                    HUNTSMAN
I'm certain. I've known this family for many years. We must find Snow White immediately.

                    MIRROR
If what you've just told us is true, it may already be too late!

> BLACKOUT. LIGHTS rise on cottage.
> THE DWARVES stand around SNOW
> WHITE, who is laying on the table. There is
> a pause.

                    DWARF #1
Is she dead?

DWARF #2
No. She seems to be in a deep sleep.

DWARF #3
Can we wake her up?

DWARF #4
No. I've tried everything I can think of.
 (Tickles HER feet. No response.)

DWARF #5
 (Picking up half eaten kumquat.)
What's this?

DWARF #6
It's a half eaten kumquat!

DWARF #7
Oh no! It's the old poison kumquat trick! I've seen it a million times!

DWARVES ALL agree.

DWARF #1
This is the work of the Evil Queen, I'll guarantee it!

HUNTSMAN
 (Entering.)
You're right, but we might be able to save her still.

DWARF #1
Who are you?

HUNTSMAN
I'm the Huntsman, and this is Prince.

DWARF #2
Oh, we've heard of you.

HUNTSMAN
So, she's in a deep sleep?

DWARF #3
It seems that way.

HUNTSMAN
Then only one thing can awaken her. The kiss of her one true love.

DWARVES look at PRINCE.

PRINCE
Don't look at me. She's my sister.

DWARVES
SAY WHAT???

HUNTSMAN
It's true. Snow White had a brother who was raised by her Uncle in the Kingdoms to the North.

DWARF #4
All is lost then.

There is a pause.

DWARF #1
Maybe not.

DWARF #1 bends over HER and kisses HER gently. SHE stirs. Then puts HER arms around HIM and plants one on HIM. DWARVES cheer. Finally HE breaks free and SHE rises.

SNOW WHITE
What happened?

HUNTSMAN
The Evil Queen cast a spell over you Princess. Only the kiss of your one true love has awakened you.

> SNOW WHITE looks at PRINCE. HE shakes HIS head no. EVERYONE points to DWARF #1. HE blushes.

SNOW WHITE
Well, I always did like older men.

DWARF #5
We're not going to let the Evil Queen get away with this are we?

SNOW WHITE
(Rising.)
Oh no. No more Miss Nice Princess. It's time for Snow White to Strike Back!

> BLACKOUT. LIGHTS rise on MIRROR and QUEEN.

QUEEN
Magic Mirror on the wall, who's the fairest of them all?

MIRROR
"You gave it your all you wicked Queen, but Snow White is coming to kick you're...
(Tries to think of a rhyme, but can't.)
...butt!"

QUEEN
Snow White? How is that even possible?

SNOW WHITE
(Who has entered.)
Oh, it's possible Stepmother!

> QUEEN turns to find SNOW WHITE

> holding green bladed sword. SHE grabs a
> red bladed sword.

QUEEN
The Dwarves have taught you well Snow White.

SNOW WHITE
They have.

QUEEN
Is it a final showdown that you're looking for Princess?

SNOW WHITE
Darn tootin!

QUEEN
Then...so be it!

> ADVENTURE MUSIC. There is a massive
> battle between THE QUEEN and SNOW
> WHITE. At one point, SNOW WHITE even
> pretends that HER hand has been cut off.
> Finally, SNOW WHITE gains both swords
> and chases THE QUEEN offstage. THE
> QUEEN screams loudly. Beat.

MIRROR
And so, with the Evil Queen vanquished, and peace restored to the Kingdom, Prince went on to become a music superstar, winning numerous Grammies and finally changing his name to a weird unpronounceable symbol.
(PRINCE enters, blows audience a kiss.)
Snow White married her true love, _____, and ironically, they had seven children of their own.
> (SNOW WHITE and DWARF #1 enter holding
> hands.)

MIRROR (Cont'd)
No one in the Kingdom ever touched another kumquat as long as they lived, and finally, there was a large celebration in the castle in which everybody got down with their bad selves.

> CAST enters. FESTIVE MUSIC. The CAST dances.
>
> THE END

Cinderella and the Quest for the Crystal Pump

(Small Cast Version)

BY

L. HENRY DOWELL

BLACK BOX THEATRE PUBLISHING

CAST

Cinderella
Prince Charming
Touchstone the Jester
Magic Mirror
Stepmother
Grizelda
Brumhilda
Fairy Godperson
Clockwork Cindy
Old Professor
Master Fuzzy
2 Spiders

Cinderella and the Quest for the Crystal Pump
(Small Cast Version)

SCENE ONE

LIGHTS: Rise to reveal a beautiful palace.

MUSIC: Classical style fairy tale music plays.

> TOUCHSTONE THE JESTER enters looking around.

TOUCHSTONE
Prince? Yoo-hoo! Prince Charming, where are you?
> (Notices audience.)

Oh, hello there. Have you seen the Prince anywhere? My goodness, that boy is always running off!
> (Resumes looking.)

Prince Charming?

> PRINCE enters, more zero than hero.

PRINCE
What is it Touchstone?

TOUCHSTONE
There you are! Where have you been? Don't you know what today is?

PRINCE
Yes, I am well aware of what today is.

TOUCHSTONE
Your birthday!
> (Blows kazoo.)

Where were you anyway? You should be getting ready for your masquerade ball!

PRINCE
I don't want to go to the masquerade ball. I was reading.

TOUCHSTONE
Reading?

PRINCE
That's right. I was reading. I just wanted to find a nice quiet little corner of the castle where no one would bother me and read for a while. Surely that isn't a bad thing?

TOUCHSTONE
Certainly not. Reading is a fine thing. Many people read. In fact I do it on occasion myself.

PRINCE
You do?

TOUCHSTONE
Of course I do.
        (Remembering.)
I got you a gift!

HE exits running.

PRINCE
That's really nice of you.

TOUCHSTONE
        (Entering, pushing a very large gift.)
I think you are going to be most surprised with this gift. It's something very special.

PRINCE
Is it that new set of encyclopedias I asked for?

TOUCHSTONE
No. How are encyclopedias something very special?

PRINCE
They're special to me.

TOUCHSTONE
(To audience.)
Before he opens his gift, shouldn't we sing a certain song? Will you help us sing for Prince Charming? You will? Fantastic! Happy Birthday to you! Happy Birthday to you! Happy Birthday Prince Charming! Happy Birthday to you! Now open your gift!

> PRINCE starts to tear open wrapping paper to reveal the head of the MAGIC MIRROR.

MIRROR
Here's Johnny!

PRINCE
Wow. It's furniture. That talks.

TOUCHSTONE
It's a mirror!

PRINCE
I can see that.

TOUCHSTONE
It's a magic mirror!

PRINCE
Just what I've always wanted.

TOUCHSTONE
I found it at a garage sale!

PRINCE
Went all out huh?

TOUCHSTONE
Evidently it has quite a bit of history attached to it. It once belonged to an evil Queen.

PRINCE
This just keeps getting better.

TOUCHSTONE
The mirror seems quite articulate.

MIRROR
That's me!

TOUCHSTONE
And extremely intelligent. Watch this. Magic Mirror on the wall, who's the fairest one of all?

MIRROR
(To the audience.)
Not this again!
(Clears throat.)
You O'Jester are the fairest in the land!

TOUCHSTONE
Oooooo, I just love this thing!

PRINCE
You keep it then.

TOUCHSTONE
No. It's your gift. Besides, it says other things too! Watch this. Magic Mirror on the wall, will the Prince enjoy his masquerade ball?

MIRROR
As I see it, yes.

TOUCHSTONE
Will there be cake at this elegant masquerade ball?

                    MIRROR
Most likely.

                    PRINCE
Is that all you care about? Cake?

                    MIRROR
It is decidedly so.

                         THEY look at the MIRROR who just
                         smiles.

                    PRINCE
Touchstone, thank you for your gift. It is a most unusual treasure, but the last thing I want is for someone to throw a ball!

                         TOUCHSTONE throws a ball into the
                         audience.

                    TOUCHSTONE
What? It's a sight gag. I'm a jester. It's my job. Besides, if you stay cooped up here in the castle all the time, how in the world will you ever have any adventures?

                    PRINCE
Adventures are overrated.

                    TOUCHSTONE
How will you ever meet any girls?

                    PRINCE
Girls are overrated too.

                         TOUCHSTONE and MIRROR look at
                         EACH OTHER.

                    TOUCHSTONE
You aren't getting any younger, you know.

PRINCE
What do you mean? I'm only 38!

TOUCHSTONE
Charles Edward Tiberius Charming III!

PRINCE
Charlie.

TOUCHSTONE
What?

PRINCE
I prefer to be called Charlie.

TOUCHSTONE
Since when?

PRINCE
It's my birthday. I can go by whatever name I want.

TOUCHSTONE
That's ridiculous. Who ever heard of a Prince named Charlie Charming?

PRINCE
(Turns to MIRROR.)
Mirror…what do you think? Will I find the "right" girl at this masquerade ball?

MIRROR
Reply hazy. Try again later.

PRINCE

That figures.
>(To audience.)

Aw gee whiz! The "right" girl? What does that mean anyway? No "left" girls? What does the "right" girl look like? Would I know her if I ran into her on the street? No. I'm not ready for this. I'm afraid of girls. I know! I'll run far, far away!

TOUCHSTONE

You can't! The masquerade ball! You can't just run away!

PRINCE

Of course I can.
>(Thinking.)

Come with me Touchstone!

TOUCHSTONE

What? Out there?

PRINCE

Why not?

TOUCHSTONE

But…I'm a Jester? I've been a Jester my whole life. What would I do out there? In the real world!

PRINCE

Who knows? Go in to politics maybe.

TOUCHSTONE

If we go…and we don't like it…can we ever come back?

PRINCE

I honestly don't know.

TOUCHSTONE

Ok. I'll do it. Just so I can watch over you.

MIRROR
Hey guys?

PRINCE
Mirror?

MIRROR
Can I go too?

PRINCE
You want to come with us?

MIRROR
Sure. It beats hanging around here all the time.
  (Laughs way too long and way too hard.)

PRINCE
Yes. That's a good one. I guess with your ability to tell fortunes you might come in handy. But you can tell us the answer better than anybody…Magic Mirror…would it be to our advantage to take you along?

MIRROR
Ask again later.

PRINCE
What?

MIRROR
Better not tell you now!

PRINCE
What?

MIRROR
Most likely?

  THEY give HER a look.

MIRROR
Yes!

PRINCE
Ok. Good. Now if we are going out into the real world, we are going to need some disguises.

TOUCHSTONE
I have just the thing right here.
    (Pulls mustaches out of pocket.)

PRINCE
Fake mustaches?

TOUCHSTONE
Yep!

    THEY put them on. MIRROR too.

PRINCE
And we're off to find a life completely devoid of any adventure whatsoever and absolutely no girls!

ALL
Absolutely no girls!!!

    LIGHTS: BLACKOUT.

SCENE TWO

LIGHTS: Rise on Cinderella's cottage. CINDERELLA enters wearing work clothes. SHE sweeps and seems happy.

STEPMOTHER
(Offstage.)
Cinderella? Are you finished with that sweeping yet?

CINDERELLA
Not yet Stepmother!

BRUMHILDA
(Offstage.)
Cinderella? Did you get that laundry done? I can't find my purple bloomers!

CINDERELLA
Not yet Brumhilda!

GRIZELDA
(Offstage.)
Cinderella! Don't forget to beat the rugs!

CINDERELLA
Will do Grizelda!

STEPMOTHER
And feed the fish!

BRUMHILDA
And milk the cow!

GRIZELDA
And mow the grass!

STEPMOTHER
And clean the gutters!

BRUMHILDA
And take out the trash!

GRIZELDA
And churn the buttermilk!

STEPMOTHER, BRUMHILDA and GRIZELDA
Cinderella!!!

CINDERELLA
Yes! I heard you! I'll get everything done I promise.
(To audience.)
Gee whiz! My life is so bland and boring! I just can't stand it sometimes! "Cinderella, do the dishes!" "Cinderella, beat the rugs!" "Cinderella, fold the laundry!" "Cinderella, churn the buttermilk!" I hate buttermilk. Am I crazy for wanting to know what's out...there? Beyond these walls?

STEPMOTHER enters.

STEPMOTHER
Cinderella. Come and sit here beside me.
(THEY sit at table.)
I know you have a lot of work to do.

CINDERELLA
Yes ma'am! I certainly do.

STEPMOTHER
Things have been difficult ever since your beloved father disappeared.

CINDERELLA
I know.

STEPMOTHER
I want to do something to help you get all of chores done.

CINDERELLA
That would be wonderful! Thank you so much!

STEPMOTHER
I want to give you some advice.

CINDERELLA
Advice?

STEPMOTHER
You must learn to manage your time better my dear. Multi-task. Learn to do two things at once. Like beating the rugs and churning the buttermilk at the same time. You do have two hands you know. Do you understand me Cinderella?

CINDERELLA
I think so.

STEPMOTHER
Good. I'm glad we had this little talk. Now get back to work!
(CINDERELLA resumes cleaning.
STEPMOTHER addresses audience.)
Have you ever noticed the bias in these stories against stepmothers? I just want to go on the record here as being against this sort of negative stereotyping. Stepmothers have a very difficult job you know. Blending two separate families together into one cohesive unit is tough enough, and when you factor in the mysterious disappearance of my husband Henry. He was a famous explorer you know. Well, that sort of thing is apt to make any woman…grouchy. You know what I mean? It's not that I dislike Cinderella…

CINDERELLA
Stepmother, would you…

STEPMOTHER
(Yelling.)
In a minute Cinderella! Can't you see I'm doing my monologue!

CINDERELLA

Oh. Sorry.

STEPMOTHER

Where was I? Oh yes. It's not that I really dislike Cinderella. She just...I don't know...annoys the living crap out of me with all her sweetness! All her "pleases" and "thank yous" and "yes ma'ams". I bet she was an honor roll student too.

CINDERELLA

I was.

> (STEPMOTHER shoots HER a look.)

Sorry.

STEPMOTHER

Anyway...my point is, that it's a very difficult job and people shouldn't be so quick to judge us stepmothers, at least not till you've walked a mile in my expensive and highly fashionable footwear.

> SOUND: Doorbell rings. BRUMHILDA enters.

BRUMHILDA

Someone's at the door.

> SOUND: Doorbell rings. GRIZELDA enters.

GRIZELDA

Anybody going to get the door?

> THEY look at CINDERELLA.

CINDERELLA

I'll get the door.

> SHE exits, then re-enters with scroll.

CINDERELLA

By order of the Royal Family…an elegant masquerade ball will be held Saturday next in celebration of the birthday of Prince Charles Edward Tiberius Charming! All eligible maidens living in the kingdom are hereby invited to attend.

STEPMOTHER

A ball?

BRUMHILDA

A ball?

GRIZELDA

A ball?

CINDERELLA

A masquerade ball, to be precise.

STEPMOTHER

Anything in that notice about an age limit?

CINDERELLA

No.

STEPMOTHER

Hot dog! We are going to the big dance girls!

BRUMHILDA

Excuse me?

GRIZELDA

Did you just say "we"?

STEPMOTHER

That's right. "We". Maybe the Prince's taste in women runs to the ever so slightly more mature.

BRUMHILDA and GRIZELDA

Bwah-ha-ha-ha-ha!

STEPMOTHER shoots THEM a look.
THEY shut up.

STEPMOTHER
Let's face it. When you've got it, you've got it.

BRUMHILDA
I'm going to look gorgeous! There's no way the Prince will be able to resist me!

GRIZELDA
Are you kidding? He'll take one look at me and forget your name!

BRUMHILDA
He's mine! You hear me?

GRIZELDA
Over my dead body!

BRUMHILDA
That can be arranged you know!

GRIZELDA
Mother! Brumhilda just threatened me!

STEPMOTHER
I don't care. Just don't get any blood on the floor. Cinderella is far too busy to clean it up.
 (Paces.)
Oh girls! There's so much to do! We have to find dresses and get our hair done...

CINDERELLA
Stepmother?

STEPMOTHER
Yes Cinderella? What is it?

CINDERELLA
May I go to the masquerade ball too?

STEPMOTHER
Excuse me?

CINDERELLA
I never get to go anywhere. It would only be for one night.

BRUMHILDA
Poor Cinderella!

GRIZELDA
She seems to think she'd have a chance at nabbing the Prince for herself!

STEPMOTHER BRUMHILDA, and GRIZELDA
Bwah-ha-ha-ha-ha!

STEPMOTHER
Is that true Cinderella? Do you think the Prince might fancy a girl as plain and ordinary as yourself?

CINDERELLA
Oh no. Of course not. It's not that at all. I would just like to get out of here for a while.

STEPMOTHER
Well, I suppose you could go, provided you can find a suitable dress. I will not have you embarrassing us by showing up at the royal palace in rags!

CINDERELLA
Of course not.

STEPMOTHER
You'll have to get all of your chores done first.

CINDERELLA
Yes Ma'am.

STEPMOTHER
Very well. Come girls! We must go shopping!

BRUMHILDA and GRIZELDA
Shopping!

> THEY exit. CINDERELLA turns to the audience.

CINDERELLA
I just want to get out of here. See the world beyond these four walls. I want to travel and meet people. All kinds of people. I want to have adventures! I want to go to that ball! Is that too much to wish for?

> THE FAIRY GODPERSON appears in a puff of smoke and music.

FAIRY GODPERSON
Why, no my dear. Not too much at all.

CINDERELLA
Who are you...and how did you get in here?

FAIRY GODPERSON
I am your Fairy Godperson. I go where I wish.

CINDERELLA
Fairy God "person"?

FAIRY GODPERSON
It's the world we live in my dear. Even the Fairy Tales are getting all politically correct.

CINDERELLA
Why are you here?

FAIRY GODPERSON
I am here to grant your fondest wish.

CINDERELLA
Really?

FAIRY GODPERSON
Hey, would I lie?

CINDERELLA
I don't know. I just met you.

FAIRY GODPERSON
Oh, I'm very honest. Take my word for it.

CINDERELLA
And you are here to grant my fondest wish?

FAIRY GODPERSON
Indeed. I'm a Fairy Godperson, it's what I do.

CINDERELLA
That's fantastic!

FAIRY GODPERSON
I thought you'd like that...and just what is your fondest wish Cinderella?

CINDERELLA
I wish to go to the ball!

FAIRY GODPERSON
The masquerade ball that they're throwing at the palace?

CINDERELLA
That's the one.

FAIRY GODPERSON
I see. You'll need a dress of course.

CINDERELLA

Of course.

FAIRY GODPERSON

A fabulous dress.

CINDERELLA

Please!

FAIRY GODPERSON

And we have to do something about your hair!

CINDERELLA

I figured.

FAIRY GODPERSON

And shoes!

CINDERELLA

Shoes?

FAIRY GODPERSON

You'll need some new shoes!

CINDERELLA

I do love new shoes!

FAIRY GODPERSON

Who doesn't? And we are not talking about any old shoes!

CINDERELLA

Oh no?

FAIRY GODPERSON

Oh no! For this you'll need the perfect shoes to accentuate that cute little footsie of yours! A pair of shoes befitting a Princess!

CINDERELLA

A Princess?

FAIRY GODPERSON

Indeed! For this you will require nothing less than the perfect pair of Crystal Pumps!

CINDERELLA

Oh my!!!

FAIRY GODPERSON

You will have to earn these things Cinderella!

CINDERELLA

But how?

FAIRY GODPERSON

You must go on a quest! It won't be easy!

CINDERELLA

My father used to say that "nothing worth having ever is". Easy that is.

FAIRY GODPERSON

Your father sounds like a wise man.

CINDERELLA

He is. Was. He was a famous explorer. He disappeared mysteriously some years ago.

FAIRY GODPERSON

Do not trouble yourself with such things now. Keep your mind on the adventure at hand. And it will be a grand adventure, Cinderella.

CINDERELLA

But what about my Stepmother? Won't she miss me? She'll never agree to let me go to the ball once she learns I've run away on this "grand adventure".

FAIRY GODPERSON
Hmmmm. I hadn't thought of that. I have an idea though.

> HE pulls out a cell phone.

CINDERELLA
What's that?

FAIRY GODPERSON
This is a cell phone. They'll be very big one day. I'm shopping online.

CINDERELLA
Online?

FAIRY GODPERSON
You'll see.

> SOUND: DOORBELL.

FAIRY GODPERSON
That'll be our order!

CINDERELLA
That was fast.

FAIRY GODPERSON
I paid extra for fast shipping. Cinderella, we are going to replace you.

CINDERELLA
Replace me?

FAIRY GODPERSON
Allow me to introduce the latest technological marvel...
> (HE pulls out a remote control, and twists some knobs. CLOCKWORK CINDY enters. She is a robotic version of CINDERELLA.)

...the Cinderella 3000...or Clockwork Cindy for short!

CINDERELLA
Clockwork Cindy?

FAIRY GODPERSON
She'll be the perfect stand in for you. No one will suspect a thing.

CINDERELLA
Can she talk?

FAIRY GODPERSON
Can she talk? What a question! Can she talk!
> (Beat.)
I think she can talk. Let's find out.

> HE flips some switches.

CLOCKWORK CINDY
I want to rule the world! Bwah-ha-ha-ha-ha!

FAIRY GODPERSON
Oops! Wrong setting.

> HE makes an adjustment to CLOCKWORK CINDY, and then pushes a button.

CLOCKWORK CINDY
I love to clean.
> (Pause.)
I love to bake.
> (Pause.)
Oooo is that a new broom?

CINDERELLA
I don't sound like that.

FAIRY GODPERSON
Sure you do. Don't worry about a thing Cinderella.

CINDERELLA
Ok. I guess I'm on my way then.

FAIRY GODPERSON
Don't forget, you have to be back home by midnight.

CINDERELLA
Why midnight?

FAIRY GODPERSON
This is a school performance honey. If these little kids have to sit here too long, they'll pee in their seats, and we don't want that.

CINDERELLA
No! Nobody wants that!
(Starts to go.)
Goodbye!

FAIRY GODPERSON
Goodbye Cinderella! And good luck!

SHE exits.

LIGHTS: BLACKOUT.

SCENE THREE

LIGHTS: Rise on a street scene. CINDERELLA enters on one side reading a map. PRINCE enters on the other side reading a map, followed by MIRROR, and TOUCHSTONE. PRINCE and CINDERELLA run into EACH OTHER.

PRINCE and CINDERELLA
Oh. Sorry.

PRINCE
It was my fault. I'm such a klutz.

CINDERELLA
No. I should watch where I'm going.

PRINCE
Where were you going?

CINDERELLA
Pardon?

PRINCE
My friends and I are kind of lost.

CINDERELLA
Me too I'm afraid. I'm sorry, I didn't catch your name?

PRINCE
It's…Charlie. My name is Charlie.
(To MIRROR.)
This is my friend…Mario.

MIRROR
Hiya!

PRINCE
(To TOUCHSTONE.)
And this is his brother…Luigi.

TOUCHSTONE
Lets a go!

CINDERELLA
Those are very interesting names.

TOUCHSTONE
Don't blame us. We didn't pick 'em.

TOUCHSTONE and MIRROR give
PRINCE a dirty look.

CINDERELLA
My name's Cinderella. I'm very pleased to meet all of you.

PRINCE
The pleasure is all ours. Listen, my friends and I, we're not from around here. Do you think that maybe we could tag along with you for a while?

CINDERELLA
I don't know. I'm kind of on a quest.

PRINCE
A quest? Really? For what?

CINDERELLA
Shoes…I guess you could say.

PRINCE
Shoes?
(To HIMSELF.)
That sounds pretty boring!
(To CINDERELLA.)
We'd love to come along with you on your quest if it's ok with you Cinderella.

CINDERELLA
I suppose it would be all right. I'm searching for the perfect pair of Crystal Pumps.

PRINCE
Sounds fancy.

CINDERELLA
I'm going to the masquerade ball. I want to look my best.

PRINCE
The masquerade ball at the palace? Oh…that sounds like great fun.

CINDERELLA
I hope so. Every maiden in the kingdom will be there.

PRINCE
Probably.

CINDERELLA
I wonder what the Prince is really like. He's probably a total jerk.

TOUCHSTONE and MIRROR snicker.

PRINCE
I hear he's a pretty nice guy. Isn't that right…Mario? Luigi?

MIRROR
Whatever you say boss.

TOUCHSTONE

Let's a go!

CINDERELLA

I have no idea what I'd even say to the Prince if I did meet him. "What's shaking Prince?" "How 'bout them Mets?"

PRINCE

Maybe you could just start out with "Hi. My name is Cinderella. Pleased to meet you."

CINDERELLA

Yeah. That might work. I'll remember that if it ever happens, which right now is very doubtful.

TOUCHSTONE

Oh, I don't know. I'd say the odds are better than you think.

CINDERELLA

You think so?

MIRROR

You may rely on it.

PRINCE

So where is this Crystal Pump that you are looking for?

CINDERELLA

According to this map, it's over the river and across the green.

PRINCE

Kind of a funny place for a shoe store, but what are we waiting on?
    (To MIRROR and TOUCHSTONE.)
Guys?

MIRROR and TOUCHSTONE

Let's a go!

THEY EXIT.

LIGHTS: BLACKOUT.

SCENE FOUR

LIGHTS: Rise on a forest scene. CINDERELLA, PRINCE, MIRROR, and TOUCHSTONE enter slowly, looking around.

TOUCHSTONE
Wh...where are we?

CINDERELLA
According to this map, we are in the Black Forest.

PRINCE
And just why are we in such a scary place when we are supposed to be shoe shopping?

TOUCHSTONE
I thought we were going to the mall.

MIRROR
Me too. I wanted a slurpee.

CINDERELLA
Evidently there's something here that will show us the way to the Crystal Pumps.

PRINCE
These better be some awesome shoes!

CINDERELLA
Oh they are! I know it. They just have to be!

TOUCHSTONE
Look! Someone's coming. Someone really short.

MASTER FUZZY enters. Very Yoda-ish.

CINDERELLA
Uh...hi? Could you help us?

MASTER FUZZY
To me talking you are?

CINDERELLA
Yes. I think. Huh?

MASTER FUZZY
My counsel seek you?

TOUCHSTONE
Wow! This guy's grammar sucks.

MASTER FUZZY
Heard that I did!

TOUCHSTONE
Uh…sorry I am.

CINDERELLA
This map led me here. It was given to me by my Fairy Godperson. I'm looking for…

MASTER FUZZY
Know I what you seek. The Cavern of the Crystal Pump.

PRINCE
Cavern? Who puts a show store in a cave?

CINDERELLA
(To PRINCE.)

Shhhh.

(To MASTER FUZZY.)

Yes. We seek the way and we were hoping that you could help us…

MASTER FUZZY
Master Fuzzy my name is, and help you I will.

CINDERELLA, PRINCE, TOUCHSTONE, and MIRROR

YAY!!!

MASTER FUZZY

After test you pass.

CINDERELLA, PRINCE, TOUCHSTONE and MIRROR

HUH???

MASTER FUZZY

Worthy you must be. Prove it you must.

TOUCHSTONE

We're quite worthy I assure you, this guy is…

PRINCE elbows HIM.

PRINCE

…wondering what we might have to do to prove our worth Master Fuzzy?

MASTER FUZZY

Battle you must.

MIRROR

Oh poop!

TOUCHSTONE

I'm a lover! Not a fighter!

PRINCE

You want us to battle?

MASTER FUZZY

Repeat myself I will not.

CINDERELLA
You really want us to fight to prove ourselves to you?

MASTER FUZZY
Repeat myself I will not.

TOUCHSTONE
But you just…

>   PRINCE elbows HIM again.

PRINCE
Ok then. If you want us to battle…we'll battle.

>   HE grabs TOUCHSTONE and puts HIM in a headlock. THEY all battle EACH OTHER.

MASTER FUZZY
Morons.
    (THEY stop.)
Among yourselves do not fight.

CINDERELLA
Then who do we battle?

MASTER FUZZY
Me.

>   MUSIC: BATTLE MUSIC. Large fight. Eventually only CINDERELLA remains. MASTER FUZZY claps.

MASTER FUZZY
Most impressive Cinderella.

CINDERELLA
Thank you. Will you help us now?

MASTER FUZZY

I will.

CINDERELLA

How do we get to the Cavern of the Crystal Pump?

MASTER FUZZY

No idea have I.

CINDERELLA

What? You have no idea?

MASTER FUZZY

Nope.

CINDERELLA

Then what was all of this for?

MASTER FUZZY

Enjoy a good fight do I.

CINDERELLA

Thanks for nothing. Let's go guys.

MASTER FUZZY

Wait! Know the way I do not. Know the way to the one who knows the way I do.

TOUCHSTONE

Huh?

MASTER FUZZY

Seek you the one who went before. Aid you on your quest, this will.
    (Hands compass to CINDERELLA.)

CINDERELLA

It's a compass.

MASTER FUZZY
So observant, you are. To your hearts fondest desire, it will lead.

MASTER FUZZY exits. THEY start to exit.

PRINCE
Where are we going Cinderella?

CINDERELLA
I'm not sure…but evidently we are going to find out.

THEY exit.

LIGHTS: BLACKOUT.

SCENE FIVE

LIGHTS: Rise dimly on cave. Lots of fog.

MUSIC: MARIO CASTLE MUSIC.

> CINDERELLA, PRINCE, TOUCHSTONE, and MIRROR enter.

MIRROR
We made it. The Cavern of the Crystal Pump!

TOUCHSTONE
How do you know this is the right cave?

MIRROR
There's a sign over there that says "Welcome to The Cavern of the Crystal Pump".

> THEY look and sure enough, there's the sign.

ALL
Oh yeah! Look at that! There is a sign! Etc!

TOUCHSTONE
This place is really spooky!

PRINCE
You can say that again.

TOUCHSTONE
This place is really spooky!

PRINCE
How did I know you were going to say that?

TOUCHSTONE
That's me. A reliable source of comic shtick! Would you like to see me slip on a banana peel?

PRINCE
No.

CINDERELLA
What's that over there?

> SHE crosses to a wall and takes a parchment from it and blows off the dust.

PRINCE
What is it?

CINDERELLA
It looks like a riddle.
  (Reads.)
I run over fields and woods all day
Under the bed at night I sit alone
My tongue hangs out, up and to the rear
Waiting to be filled in the morning
What am I?

> LIGHTS: Rise to reveal letters on the floor.

MIRROR
Look! On the ground! Letters of some sort!

TOUCHSTONE
What could it all mean?

CINDERELLA
Shoes!

PRINCE
Shoes?

TOUCHSTONE

Shoes?

MIRROR

Shoes?

TOUCHSTONE

Of course, shoes begin with the letter "S"!

> HE steps on the letter "S". There is a rumbling. 2 GIANT SPIDERS enter and chase THEM.

CINDERELLA

No Luigi, the riddle is written in ancient Hebrew, and everybody knows that in ancient Hebrew the word for shoe begins with an "N".

PRINCE

You can read ancient Hebrew?

CINDERELLA

Of course. My father taught me.

PRINCE

Impressive.

OLD PROFESSOR
(From offstage.)
I agree. It is impressive. You have learned your lessons well!

> HE enters. Very old and grey. Wearing a fedora and a leather jacket.

CINDERELLA

Father?

OLD PROFESSOR

It's me Cindy.

CINDERELLA
When you didn't come back we assumed you'd been killed.

OLD PROFESSOR
Dead? No. Just trapped in this cave by those giant spiders.

CINDERELLA
How did you survive all this time?

OLD PROFESSOR
Dried kumquats.

CINDERELLA
What's a kumquat?

OLD PROFESSOR
A kumquat is a subtropical, pulpy citrus fruit, used chiefly for preserves.

CINDERELLA
I never knew that.

MIRROR
I did.

OLD PROFESSOR
I always pack my pockets full of them when I'm on a quest. Would you like some?

CINDERELLA
Uh…no. I ate before I left.

OLD PROFESSOR
Cindy. I've got to know. Your Stepmother…is she still the same sweet, lovable girl I left behind?

CINDERELLA
No Father…she's been sort of grumpy since you disappeared to tell you the truth.

OLD PROFESSOR
I can't wait to see her again. That is, if we ever get out of here.

CINDERELLA
We'll get out of here together Father.

OLD PROFESSOR
How will we? We can't go back now.

CINDERELLA
That's all right. I'm not leaving without the Crystal Pumps.

OLD PROFESSOR
Like father, like daughter. But if we're going to do this, Cinderella, then let's do it right.
(Pulls out a fedora.)
Welcome to the family business.

> HE places the fedora on HER head.
> MUSIC: INDIANA JONES THEME.
> There are a series of small scenes depicting the GROUP tip toeing across the floor. Running from SPIDERS. Taking a dance break, running, ducking, covering, and finally removing, slowly, the CRYSTAL PUMP from a podium and replacing it with a TV. THEY look around. Nothing. THEY smile and congratulate EACH OTHER. Then there is smoke and SPIDERS. THEY all run crazily in all directions.
>
> LIGHTS: BLACKOUT.

SCENE SIX

LIGHTS: Rise on palace. STEPMOTHER, BRUMHILDA and GRIZELDA are tied up. CINDERELLA enters.

CINDERELLA
Stepmother? What happened?

SHE unties THEM.

STEPMOTHER
It was Cinderella...the other Cinderella...she's evil. At first we thought she was you...

BRUMHILDA
But then she was all like "Do this!" and "Do that!"

GRIZELDA
Sweep the floor!

BRUMHILDA
Beat the rugs!

STEPMOTHER
And churn the buttermilk! Oh, how I hate buttermilk!

STEPMOTHER, BRUMHILDA and GRIZELDA
Buttermilk!!!

THEY start bawling.

CINDERELLA
Stepmother. I found someone. I think you might know him.

OLD PROFESSOR enters.

STEPMOTHER
Henry? Is that you?

OLD PROFESSOR
It's me…and stop calling me that.

STEPMOTHER
Where have you been all this time?

OLD PROFESSOR
Trapped in the Cavern of the Crystal Pump by a bunch of giant man eating spiders.

STEPMOTHER
How did you keep from going mad?

OLD PROFESSOR
I did what any man would do in that situation. I tried on women's shoes.

STEPMOTHER
You poor thing!

OLD PROFESSOR
I'll never understand how you women can walk in those blasted things!

STEPMOTHER
Oh Henry!

OLD PROFESSOR
I told you to stop calling me Henry!

STEPMOTHER
But that's your name.

OLD PROFESSOR
I prefer to be called…"Indiana"!

STEPMOTHER
But honey, we named the dog Indiana!!!

ALL laugh.

CLOCKWORK CINDY enters.

CINDERELLA
Clockwork Cindy!

CLOCKWORK CINDY
My name is Cinderella. I love to cook.

CINDERELLA
No. My name is Cinderella! You are nothing but a fake!

CLOCKWORK CINDY
I love to clean!

CINDERELLA
Stop that!

CLOCKWORK CINDY
Is that a new broom?

CINDERELLA
Ok, that's it! It's time for Cinderella to clean house!

BATTLE MUSIC. THEY remove THEIR shoes, then battle. Evenly matched. Just when it seems CINDERELLA is finished, the PRINCE enters, wearing a mask. HE fights CLOCKWORK CINDY.

STEPMOTHER
Who is that?

TOUCHSTONE and MIRROR
It's Prince Charming!

BRUMHILDA

Prince Charming?

GRIZELDA

Prince Charming?

CINDERELLA

Prince Charming?

PRINCE

That's right!
> (Hands CINDERELLA her sword.)

Here's your sword Cinderella.

CINDERELLA

You know my name? How?

PRINCE

Everybody knows the daughter of the world's most famous explorer! Nice shoes by the way!

CINDERELLA

Thanks!

> THEY continue to fight until CLOCKWORK CINDY is vanquished.

TOUCHSTONE

Prince Charming! We are so proud of you!

PRINCE

Thank you.

> SOUND: CLOCK STRIKES MIDNIGHT.

CINDERELLA

Oh no! Midnight! My time is up!

> SHE starts to run out.

PRINCE
Wait Cinderella. I need to tell you something.

CINDERELLA
I can't stay. Please. It's not you. It's me.

CAST
Groan!

CINDERELLA
I think you are a very nice guy and a pretty good swordsman and all, but you see, I'm in love with someone else.

PRINCE
What?

CINDERELLA
I wanted to come here and meet you, but along the way I met another guy. I need to go find him and tell him how I feel.

PRINCE
I see. Do what you must, but don't forget these.

HE hands HER the CRYSTAL PUMPS.

CINDERELLA
Thank you.

PRINCE
And don't forget this.

HE places the fedora on HER head.

CINDERELLA
How did you…?
(HE removes mask.)
Charlie? Why did….I didn't…I…Hi. My name is Cinderella. Pleased to meet you.

THEY kiss.

CINDERELLA
Your name is Charlie?

PRINCE
Yep.

CINDERELLA
Charlie Charming?

PRINCE
Yep. Interested in becoming Mrs. Charlie Charming?

CINDERELLA
I think I might keep my maiden name.

PRINCE
What's that?

CINDERELLA
Jones.

SHE winks at the audience. MIRROR comes forward.

MIRROR
And so, with peace restored to the kingdom…

FAIRY GODPERSON
(Offstage.)
Wait!

HE enters with HIS usual flourish.

CINDERELLA
It's my Fairy Godperson!

FAIRY GODPERSON
You are not narrating this show Mirror.

MIRROR
Sorry.

FAIRY GODPERSON
In fact, I think your narrating days are behind you. Magic Mirror on the wall, what's your fondest wish of all?

MIRROR
Well...I'd like to be a real girl.

FAIRY GODPERSON
Very well. Bippity-boppity...oh to heck with it. Come on out from behind the wall.

MIRROR comes out.

MIRROR
I'm a real girl! I'm a real girl!

TOUCHSTONE
Ok Pinocchio...here...
    (Hands HER a handkerchief.)
Wipe your make-up off. What about me Fairy Whatever? Do I get a wish?

FAIRY GODPERSON
Of course dear Touchstone. What do you desire most?

TOUCHSTONE
Uh..........

FAIRY GODPERSON
How about your very own HBO Comedy Special?

TOUCHSTONE
Uh..........

FAIRY GODPERSON
You're welcome.
>(To the OLD PROFESSOR and STEPMOTHER.)
And the two of you?

> THEY look at EACH OTHER.

OLD PROFESSOR and STEPMOTHER
Grandchildren!

> EVERYONE looks at PRINCE and
> CINDERELLA.

FAIRY GODPERSON
What about you Cinderella? What is your heart's fondest desire?

CINDERELLA
My wish already came true.

> SHE dips the PRINCE and kisses HIM.

FAIRY GODPERSON
And of course they all lived happily ever after. Now, is this a party or is it? Music please!

> FESTIVE MUSIC. EVERYBODY gets
> down with THEIR badselves.

THE END

THE LITTLE MERMAID
(More or Less.)

A PLAY
FOR YOUNG AUDIENCES

BY
L. HENRY DOWELL

BLACK BOX THEATRE PUBLISHING

CAST

The Director
Stagehand #1
Stagehand #2
The Lawyer
Kids #1- #5
Techie
Hippy #1
Hippy #2
Little M
Prince
Skipper
Dude
Tartar Sauce
The Crab Formerly Known As Sebastian
The Sea King
The Sea Witch
Spiro
Agnew
"The Village People"
Pierre La Frou Frou
Princess Mary Ann
Uncle Aquadude

The Little Mermaid (More or Less.)

SCENE ONE

SETTING: In the darkness, we hear familiar "mermaid" music. Suddenly the Theatre doors open and THE LAWYER enters.

LAWYER

Hold it! Stop the show! Cut the music! Lights up please!
>(MUSIC: stops. LIGHTS: come up. CAST MEMBERS poke THEIR heads out.)

Who's in charge here? Where is the director of this production?

>THE DIRECTOR comes running in. Frustrated that someone would dare mess with HIS show! HE is followed by THE STAGEHANDS.

DIRECTOR

I'm in charge here and I demand to know who you are and why you have interrupted my production?

LAWYER
>(Looking at program.)

Are you the director?

DIRECTOR

I am. And who are you?

LAWYER

I'm a lawyer.

DIRECTOR

OH POOP!

LAWYER
"Oh poop" is right.
> (Removes mouse ears from briefcase and puts them on.)

I represent a certain "mouse eared" company. Maybe you have heard of them?

DIRECTOR
Can't say that I have.

LAWYER
I see. Well, that "mouse eared" company is often ripped off by third rate Theatre groups trying to infringe on their copyrighted material.

DIRECTOR
I can assure you, we are barely third rate!

LAWYER
Excuse me?

DIRECTOR
Never mind. But you see, we're doing the Hans Christian Anderson fairy tale. Aren't we, Stagehands?
> (STAGEHANDS look at EACH OTHER confused. HE repeats louder.)

Aren't we, STAGEHANDS?

STAGEHANDS
Yep. You bet. That's right. Uh huh. Etc.

LAWYER

Well, the Little Mermaid was written by Hans Christian Anderson, that's true. But that song that was playing when I walked in, sounded an awful lot like one of the songs from our movie. I'm going to have a seat out here in the audience, and if I see any of our copyrighted material, including songs, character names, costume designs or anything else at all that resembles any material from our production, we'll slap a lawsuit on you so fast you'll wish you never heard of M-I-C-K-E-Y-M-O-U-S-E. We'll sue this Theatre for every last penny it has! That includes garnishing your salary, Mr. Director!

WHOLE CAST

GASP!

DIRECTOR

Egad! Not my salary!

LAWYER

Yes. Your salary. Do I make myself clear, Mr. Director?

DIRECTOR

Yes. You are crystal clear, Miss Lawyer.

LAWYER

Excellent. I'm going to be watching this show very closely, but first, I gotta go, and I do mean GO! Where's the little girl's room?

DIRECTOR

Gas station. Down the street.

LAWYER

Are you serious?

MR. DIRECTOR

Yep.

                    LAWYER
Classy joint you have here. Ok. I'll be right back. Don't start
the play until I come back.

                SHE starts to exit the Theatre.

                    DIRECTOR
Oh no! I wouldn't dream of it. Don't worry though, there's
nothing going on here that in any way even remotely
resembles copyright infringement.
        (Makes sure LAWYER is gone.)
Kids! Come out here quick! Hurry!

                KIDS enter from backstage.

                    KID #1
What's wrong, Mr. Director?

                    DIRECTOR
We have to get rid of everything!

                    KID #1
Why?

                    DIRECTOR
Because I said so!

                    STAGEHAND #1
Why do adults always say that?

                    STAGEHAND #2
Don't ask me.

                    DIRECTOR
We have to get rid of the music!
        (Looks at tech booth.)
Techies! Get rid of everything!

TECHIE
Are you joking?

DIRECTOR
Do I look like I'm joking?
  (Makes goofy face.)

KID #1
What will we do for music Mr. Director?

DIRECTOR
I have no idea! What do we have?

KID #1
My mom has the greatest hits of the 70's in her car!

DIRECTOR
What? Why didn't you say so? I was really cool in the 70's!

KID #1
If you say so, Mr. Director.

KID #2
Mr. Director!

DIRECTOR
Yes?

KID #2
What about the costumes?

DIRECTOR
What about the costumes?

KID #2
You made my mom watch the Little Mermaid one hundred and fourteen times so she could make the costumes look just like the costumes in the movie!

DIRECTOR
We can't use any of them now. I'm sorry!

KID #2
You are making my Mom cry, Mr. Director!

DIRECTOR
(Looks at audience.)
Sorry Mom! What else do we have that we can use?

KID #2
Just some old rags we use to clean the toilets.

KIDS
Yuck!

DIRECTOR
Toilet rags! That'll do!

> DIRECTOR and KIDS run every which way. KID #3 enters with wacky looking costume.

KID #3
I'm not wearing this, Mr. Director!

> DIRECTOR enters.

DIRECTOR
Oh yes, you are!

KID #3
Why?

DIRECTOR
Because I said so.

> KID #4 enters carrying something ridiculous.

KID #4
But Mr. Director!

DIRECTOR
Just put it on!

> KID #5 enters wearing something way too big and silly looking.

KID #5
Does anyone have any safety pins?
(Runs off.)

DIRECTOR
Is the blood sucking Lawyer back yet?

LAWYER
(Entering.)
Right here.

DIRECTOR
Oh. Excellent. So…now, on we go with our show….a show that in no way, shape or form resembles the movie of the same name. Does <u>everybody</u> understand that?

WHOLE CAST
YES, MR. DIRECTOR!

DIRECTOR
Ok everybody…action!

> LIGHTS: BLACKOUT. MUSIC. HIPPY #1 and HIPPY #2 enter.

HIPPY #1
Hey man…this is so far out!

HIPPY #2

Ah dude…..you ain't seen nothing yet man…you see, once upon a time, there was this little mermaid.
>(LITTLE M enters. SHE is very tall. SHE wears sunglasses and a leather jacket.)

HIPPY #1

Dude…there ain't nothing little about that mermaid! She's gigantic!

>LITTLE M has been smiling at the audience. Now SHE shakes HER fist at HIPPY #1.

HIPPY #1

Sorry. Anyway, her name was Ariel and….

HIPPY #2

Dude! The Director said we couldn't use that name!

HIPPY #1

Why not?

HIPPY #2

Cause you-know-who made that name up.

HIPPY #1

You-know-who?

HIPPY #2

You know…"M-I-C"…

HIPPY #1

Oh yeah... "M-I-C" You mean that wasn't her name in the book?

HIPPY #2

No way, man!

HIPPY #1

Oh….uh…then her name was…well…it was…oh, I know. She didn't have a real name. People just called her The Little Mermaid, or Little M for short. Of all the beautiful daughters of the Sea King, Little M was the youngest….er…tallest daughter. He loved her more than anything, even though she was so freakin' weird.

LITTLE M

I heard that.

HIPPY #1

Just go with it. Little M had three friends who went with her everywhere. A Sea Gull named…uh…

HIPPY #2

Think of something, dude!

HIPPY #1

Dude! That's it! The Sea Gull was named "Dude"!
    (DUDE enters.)
She also had a little yellow fish named…"Tartar Sauce".
    (TARTAR SAUCE enters.)
And a crab named…uh, a crab …I know, "A Crab Formerly Known As Sebastian"!
    (CRAB enters.)

HIPPY #2

What? What kind of name is that?

HIPPY #1

A Crab Formerly Known As Sebastian. Hey, it worked for Prince.

HIPPY #2

Who's Prince?

HIPPY #1

Never mind.

HIPPY #2
Anyway…it was about this time that Little M spotted a ship, on which stood a mighty sailor man.

> A ship enters carried by THE PRINCE and SKIPPER.

HIPPY #1
Yes, the Prince was a mighty sailor man, and the Skipper was brave and sure. They had both set sail that day for a three hour tour.

HIPPY #2
A three hour tour?

HIPPY #1
Yep. A three hour tour. But the weather started getting rough,
    (SOUND: Thunderclap.)
and the tiny ship was tossed.

> THEY shake the boat.

HIPPY #2
And so was the mighty sailor man…right over the side of the boat.

> PRINCE falls out.

HIPPY #1
Little M saw what had happened…

> SHE shrugs HER shoulders. SHE doesn't care.

LITTLE M
I don't care.

HIPPY #2
She went to rescue the man…

LITTLE M
No way. You save him.

HIPPY #1
Ahem....I said, she went to rescue the man...

LITTLE M
Nope.

HIPPY #2
Of course she had no way of knowing that the man was a Prince!

LITTLE M
What did you say? A Prince? HUBBA-HUBBA-HUBBA! Let me at him!

> MUSIC: LITTLE M pantomimes swimming over to the PRINCE, finally dragging HIM to safety. SHE performs CPR, touches HIS face tenderly, then steals HIS wallet and exits. SKIPPER has rowed the boat to THE PRINCE.

SKIPPER
Little buddy! Little Buddy! Are you alright?

PRINCE
Skipper, is that you?

SKIPPER
It's me little buddy. When you fell overboard I thought you were a goner for sure.

PRINCE
Yeah. Me too. Hey! Where's my wallet? And...what's that funky smell?

SKIPPER
Yuck! What is that?

PRINCE
It smells like.....fish!

> LIGHTS: BLACKOUT on THEM.

HIPPY #1
Days went by and the only thing that Little M could think of was the handsome Prince. She knew that mermaids were not supposed to date humans, but being the rebel that she was, she didn't care, man.

> LITTLE M enters.

LITTLE M
I don't care...man.

HIPPY #2
She knew that her father loved her deeply, so she decided to con him...I mean, to ask him for permission to date the handsome Prince.

LITTLE M
Oh, Father? Father? Where are you, oh great master of the seven seas? Oh, most noble and regal father of mine...where are you, Daddy?

> MUSIC: KING enters wearing sparkling polyester jumpsuit.

KING
Hey there, baby!

LITTLE M
Father! You look most regal! Is that a new sparkling polyester jumpsuit?

KING
Yes, it is. I think it brings out the color of my eyes. Now what brings you here? You are supposed to be preparing for your uncle's visit.

LITTLE M
I need to ask a favor of you, Father.

KING
My little daughter, you know that I adore you more than anything. There is nothing that you could ask me for that I would not give you.

LITTLE M
Can I date a human?

KING
Except that.

LITTLE M
Why not?

KING
Because.

LITTLE M
Because why?

KING
Because I said so.

LITTLE M
(Aside.)
Why do adults always say that?
(To KING.)
Is that your final word on it, Father?

KING
It is.

HE exits.

LITTLE M
(To audience.)
I'll do it anyway.

CRAB, DUDE and TARTAR SAUCE enter.
DUDE wears scuba gear, since HE is a bird
and we are underwater after all.

CRAB
You can't defy your father!

LITTLE M
Why not?

CRAB
What about your uncle's visit? He doesn't get the chance to come here very often. He stays so busy protecting the oceans from the forces of evil. Besides, how would you date a human anyhow? Humans don't last very long down here at the bottom of the ocean. Ha ha….hee hee…..get it? Humans…bottom of the ocean…get it….? Funny, right?

DUDE and TARTAR
No. Not really. Sorry. Don't quit your day job! Etc.

LITTLE M
Well then…if the mountain will not come to Muhammad, then Muhammad must go to the mountain!

DUDE
Who's Muhammad?

TARTAR
I think he was a boxer.

LITTLE M
I mean, that I must go to <u>him</u>. I will have to walk upon the land!

ALL THREE
SAY WHAT???

CRAB
Ok. Reality check. You are a mermaid. Remember? You have a tail. Humans have legs. You have no legs. Therefore you cannot walk upon land. You cannot walk upon sea. You cannot walk upon guacamole dip.
> (Starts to laugh, looks to OTHER TWO for approval. THEY shake THEIR heads no.)

LITTLE M
Well, it just so happens, I know a place where I might be able to get some legs.

CRAB
What are you talking about? Legs don't grow on trees! They don't sell legs at Wal-Mart!
> (Looks at audience.)

Not yet anyway!

LITTLE M
Well...

CRAB
What? Wait a minute...oh no! You aren't thinking what I think your thinking, are you? Because if you are thinking it, then you better quit thinking it!

DUDE
> (To TARTAR.)

What's she thinking?

CRAB
If she's thinking what I think she's thinking, then we're gonna be sinking is what I'm thinking, and that's really stinking, I'm thinking.

DUDE
(To audience.)
He's so talented.

LIGHTS: BLACKOUT. MUSIC.

HIPPY #1
Oh man! Here comes the Sea Witch! That chick is bad, man!

HIPPY #2
Dude, every story has got to have a villain.

> THE SEA WITCH enters and begins pacing. SHE has a giant afro.

WITCH
Where are they? It is so hard to find good help these days!

> SPIRO and AGNEW enter. THEY are dressed in loud suits.

WITCH
Spiro! Agnew! Where have you been? I've been waiting for you!

SPIRO
Hey boss! We been chilling!
(HE dances.)

AGNEW
We been moving and grooving!
(HE dances.)

SPIRO
Hey! Who's that coming this way?

WITCH
It's Little M. The Sea King's…tallest daughter….and some other less important supporting characters.

> LITTLE M, CRAB, TARTAR and DUDE enter.

DUDE
This place is scary.

TARTAR
You ain't just whistling Dixie.

DUDE
What's Dixie?

TARTAR
It's a song. You know, like the car horn on the Dukes of Hazzard.

DUDE
I didn't see it. I couldn't get past the whole Burt Reynolds as Boss Hogg thing. Why can't Hollywood just leave all those old 70's TV shows alone?

TARTAR
It's a lack of originality. That's what it is.

DUDE
You know, history has shown that one of the signs of a society's downfall is that they start repeating themselves artistically.

TARTAR
You mean like adapting stage plays from old animated movies?

DUDE
Yeah…something like that.

WITCH
Can I help you?

LITTLE M
Are you the Sea Witch?

WITCH
Well sugar, that's what it says on my driver's license. Who are you?
  (Aside.)
As if I didn't know.

LITTLE M
My name is Ariel….
  (DIRECTOR coughs from somewhere.)
I mean, my name is The Little Mermaid. Little M for short.

AGNEW
She don't look so little to me! Bwah-ha-ha-ha-ha!

LITTLE M
Yes. I never get tired of that joke at all.

WITCH
What brings you here?

LITTLE M
I have come to ask a favor of you.

WITCH
Well, favors don't come cheap.

LITTLE M
I figured that.

WITCH
What's the favor?

LITTLE M
I want legs.

CRAB
Legs?

TARTAR
Legs?

DUDE
Legs?

WITCH
Legs? But why? They aren't good for swimming, and you have to shave them all the time and…wait…let me guess. You have fallen in love with a human and now you want be with him upon land, but you can't because you are a mermaid, and he is a human and blah, blah, yakkity schmack!

LITTLE M
How did you know all that?

WITCH
Hey, I'm a witch. I see all. I know all. Plus the Director made me watch the movie about one hundred and fourteen times.

DIRECTOR
(From wherever.)
I did not!

LITTLE M
So, you can do it then?

WITCH
Of course I can do it. But…are you willing to pay the price?

LITTLE M

What price?

WITCH

Two things. First, you must get the Prince to kiss you before one day has passed, or you will become...

SPIRO AND AGNEW

DOM DOM DOM!

WITCH

...A TUNA!!!

LITTLE M

A tuna!

CRAB

A tuna!

TARTAR

A tuna!

DUDE

(Sings.)
A tuna ma tata!
    (HE laughs. THEY give HIM a dirty look.)
Sorry...........................Charlie.
    (HE laughs again. THEY give HIM another dirty
    look.)
I'll stop now.

LITTLE M

Why do I only have one day?

WITCH

This is Children's Theatre honey. If these kids have to sit for more than an hour, they'll pee in their seats.

LITTLE M
If I do get him to kiss me, then what?

WITCH
Then you get to keep the legs forever and ever....but wait, that's not all! I want one more thing.

SPIRO AND AGNEW
DOM DOM DOM!!!

LITTLE M
What?

WITCH
Your voice.

LITTLE M
My voice!

CRAB
Her voice!

TARTAR
Her voice!

DUDE
Her voice!

WITCH
Will you people quit that? Anyway, that's the deal. Take it or leave it.

CRAB, TARTAR, DUDE
Don't do it! No! It's a bad deal. Don't trust her! Etc.

LITTLE M
I have no choice. I love him. You have a deal.

THEY shake hands. SOUND: Thunder.

                    DUDE
How can there be thunder at the bottom of the ocean?

                    TARTAR
How can there be a seagull at the bottom of the ocean?

                    DUDE
Touché.

                    LIGHTS: BLACKOUT.

                    HIPPY #1
While all this was going down, the handsome Prince was back at the palace throwing a ball.

> LIGHTS: RISE on palace. PRINCE enters, and throws a ball.

                    HIPPY #2
Dude, I never get tired of that joke.

                    HIPPY #1
Not that kind of ball. A dance. The entertainment was provided by a group of "PEOPLE" from the local "VILLAGE."

> MUSIC: "VILLAGE PEOPLE" enter and dance. EVERYONE except PRINCE, who looks very sad. SKIPPER enters.

                    SKIPPER
Are you ok, little buddy? You look awfully sad.

                    PRINCE
Yeah Skipper. I was just sitting here thinking about that beautiful girl who saved my life. She had such a beautiful singing voice, and her face wasn't too bad either…if you catch my drift? I was hoping that she might show up tonight to my ball. HUBBA-HUBBA-HUBBA! There she is now!

PRINCE (Cont'd)
(LITTLE M has entered. HE crosses to HER.)
Hi there. You come here often?
(SHE gives HIM a look. CAST groans.)
I mean…my name is Prince Gilligan. What's your name?
(SHE makes a noise like a congested sea lion.)
Is that French?
(SHE makes the noise again.)
Oh….you can't talk, can you? I understand. I guess you aren't who I thought you were. I'm sorry to bother you.
(SHE nods YES, I AM!)
No. There's no way you could be her.
(BIG HUGE NOD. YES, I AM!)
No. Really. I know you aren't her. She had the most beautiful voice in the world. Nice try though. What are you doing here anyway?
(SHE makes a kissy face at HIM.)
I see that you are the direct type.
(She nods YES, I AM!)
I think I'll run away now.

HE does. SHE follows.

SKIPPER
(To audience.)
Some guys have all the luck!

MUSIC. Big comical chase scene.
TARTAR, CRAB and DUDE enter.
LITTLE M enters from other side.

CRAB
Well...did he kiss you?
> (SHE shakes head no.)

Did you kiss him?
> (No.)

Well, did anybody kiss anybody?
> (SHE points to the back of the audience.
> EVERYONE looks.)

Hey you two! This is Children's Theatre! Cut that out!

AUDIENCE MEMBER
Sorry.

DUDE
We have to get him to kiss you before the day is over. Wait a minute...you don't have cooties do you?
> (Shakes HER head no.)

CRAB
That's good. Wait! I have an idea!
> (Whispers to THEM.)

Now go!
> (THEY exit.)

I'll get him to kiss da girl!
> (Seems to be waiting for music to start.)

Ahem.....get it...kiss da girl!

DIRECTOR
We cut that song.

CRAB
But we rehearsed it.

DIRECTOR
No, we didn't.

CRAB
Yes, we did.

DIRECTOR
NO. WE DIDN'T. ISNEY-DAY AWYER-LAY.

CRAB
Huh-hay?
>(Gets it…finally.)

Oh….ay!

>PIERRE LA FROU FROU enters. HE is a
>FRENCH CHEF. Goofy.

CHEF
Naw…lez zee. Vat can ve hav for ze deen-air? Roast
cheekun? No. Roast peeg? No. Ah….roast crab! Ah ha-ha
oui, oui, oui!
>(Sings.)

La poison, la poison…how I love leetle feeshes….

DIRECTOR
We cut that song too.

CHEF
>(Dropping accent.)

Say what?

DIRECTOR
We cut it. Sorry.

CHEF
But Mr. Director. This was my big break! Come on. I want to
sing and dance.
>(CRAB runs to CHEF and whispers in HIS ear.)

What? Walt Who? Lawyer? Copyright infringement?
Lawsuit? Oh…I see. Ok.
>(Resumes accent.)

Ha-ha-ha-oui-oui-oui….we will have to do sometheeng
else…!

>CRAB whispers in HIS ear.

CHEF
And now Ladies and Gentlemen...another comical and time consuming chase scene!

> MUSIC: There is a very comical and time consuming chase scene. LITTLE M, DUDE, TARTAR and CRAB enter with a chair. ALL wear dental masks. PRINCE enters.

PRINCE
Hey! Look at this. A dentist! Imagine my luck. I was just saying the other day how much I needed a checkup!

> Without saying anything THEY put HIM in the chair. THEY lean HIM back. LITTLE M tries to kiss HIM. HE jumps up. A chase scene commences. In the middle of the chase scene, THEY freeze.

PRINCE
You know, I don't believe any of these people are actually licensed to practice dentistry!

> The chase resumes. THEY enter with kissing booth.

CRAB
Step right up ladies and gentlemen! Kiss the lovely girl! She's cute! She's smart! She's available!

PRINCE
Hey, look at this. A kissing booth! Imagine my luck. I was just saying the other day how much I wanted to kiss a girl in a kissing booth!

CRAB
Come on champ! Kiss the girl!

                    PRINCE
Well...ok.

                    HE starts to kiss LITTLE M, when
                    PRINCESS MARY ANN enters. SHE is
                    mad! SHE grabs PRINCE by the ear.

                    MARY ANN
What in world do you think you're doing?

                    CRAB
Who are you?

                    MARY ANN
My name is Mary Ann. I'm a princess. This is my boyfriend!

                    WHOLE CAST
BOYFRIEND???

                    LIGHTS: BLACKOUT.

                    HIPPY #1
So Little M had to return to the Sea Witch empty handed.
You see, in the Hans Christian Anderson version, the Prince
was already "attached". The Sea Witch had tricked them, and
won. So, according to their agreement, she turned Little M
into a tuna.

                    LITTLE M enters, wearing a tuna mask.
                    CRAB, TARTAR and DUDE enter.
                    WITCH, SPIRO and AGNEW enter on the
                    other side.

                    DUDE
This stinks.

                    TARTAR
You can say that again!

DUDE

This stinks.

WITCH

Take her away, boys!

SPIRO

Right on, boss!

AGNEW

Yeah! Right on!

KING
(From offstage.)

Wait!
(HE enters.)
Wait one minute here! Don't you be cruel to my little baby girl here!

WITCH

You are too late, Sea King! She and I made a deal!

KING

Well then, how about you and I make a little deal of our own, baby?

WITCH

Like what? And...did you just call me "baby"?

KING

Right on! And the deal I want to make is a trade. Me, for my daughter.

WITCH

You mean you would sacrifice yourself...and become my tuna?

KING

Yeah, baby. That's what I'm saying.

WITCH
You have yourself a deal, King Tuna!

> LITTLE M takes the mask off and hands it to KING, who puts it on.

LITTLE M
Oh, Father…No!!!

BAD GUYS
We've won! We've won!

GOOD GUYS
We've lost! We've lost!

HIPPY #1
It was then…when all hope seemed lost, that a mysterious figure suddenly appeared!

> SUPERHERO MUSIC. The Theatre doors fly open and UNCLE AQUADUDE enters.

UNCLE AQUADUDE
Wait! I'll save the day!

LITTLE M
It's my uncle! Uncle Aquadude!

> There is a dance/fight scene. At the end, UNCLE AQUADUDE has defeated the BAD GUYS.

UNCLE AQUADUDE
That's the end of those fishy fiends!

KING
(Removing mask.)
Thank you, my brother. Thank you very much!

UNCLE AQUADUDE
All in a day's work!

HIPPY #2
And that was that...and so, they all lived happ...

PRINCE
(Running in.)
Wait a minute! This story isn't over! I love you Little M!

LITTLE M
But you already have a girlfriend!

PRINCE
Not anymore. We broke up!

WHOLE CAST cheers.

CRAB
You know something...suddenly it seems just a little less roomy...

WHOLE CAST
Under the sea!

THEY look at LAWYER.

LAWYER
Ah, what the heck! Go ahead!

HIPPY #1
And so...with no danger of copyright infringement whatsoever, they all lived happily ever after...more or less.

MUSIC: EVERYONE dances, including the LAWYER.

THE END

SLEEPING BEAUTY
IN THE 25TH CENTURY

A play by L. Henry Dowell

BLACK BOX THEATRE PUBLISHING

CAST

Magic Mirror/Mr. Roboto
King
Queen
Stork
Melody/Ragged Figure #1
Arabesque/Ragged Figure #2
Thesbe/Ragged Figure #3
Evil Fairy
Princess Aurora
Rebel Commander Phillip "Buck" Rogers
Space Zombie #1
Space Zombie #2
Artists/Space Zombies

Author's Note

This play is a mash-up/parody of one of the most famous fairy tales of all time, Sleeping Beauty and the grand-daddy of all science fiction heroes, Buck Rogers and in particular, the 1979 TV series, Buck Rogers in the 25th Century. Most actors and audience members will be familiar with the former but maybe not so much with the latter. I strongly encourage cast members to view some of the TV series which is available for free online on sites like YouTube. It will be especially helpful in playing characters like Mr. Roboto, who is a parody of Twiki the Robot and Stork, who is a parody of Hawk.

Above all, these characters should be played with maximum Gusto! Theatre is supposed to be fun. If it isn't, then why bother?

SLEEPING BEAUTY IN THE 25TH CENTURY

LIGHTS: RISE on a beautiful palace and the MAGIC MIRROR.

MAGIC MIRROR
Good evening ladies and gentlemen. I am the all-seeing, all-knowing, Magic Mirror on the Wall and it is my distinct pleasure to present to you the time spanning epic, Sleeping Beauty in the 25th Century! Our tale begins as stories such as this often do, in a kingdom, far, far away! Once upon a time, in a decade known as the 70s…the 1470s that is! This particular kingdom was ruled by a benevolent King and his lovely Queen.
    (KING and QUEEN enter.)

KING
He's right you know. You really are quite lovely, my dear.

QUEEN
And you, my King are the very definition of benevolent.

MAGIC MIRROR
Benevolent. Adjective. Meaning to be kind and generous. Which was an accurate description of the King and Queen and how they ruled their kingdom. They were especially fond of the Arts and the palace was always full of dancers…
    (A DANCER enters, dancing.)
And poets…
    (A POET enters, quill in hand.)
And sculptors…
    (A SCULPTOR enters, carrying a statue.)
And musicians…
    (A MUSICIAN enters, playing an instrument.)
Painters…
    (A PAINTER enters carrying a big painting.)
And actors…

An ACTOR enters carrying a skull and sword, quoting Shakespeare.

ACTOR
To be or not to be? That is the question!

MAGIC MIRROR
I don't have the heart to tell him that Shakespeare won't be born for another 92 years. The King and Queen had everything they could possibly want…that is…except for one thing.

QUEEN
A baby!

KING
A baby!

ARTISTS
A baby!

MAGIC MIRROR
That's right, a baby. More than anything else in the world, the Queen wanted a little baby to have and to hold.

QUEEN
And to teach to sing and dance!

KING
And to sword fight!

QUEEN
Sword fight?

KING
He'll need to know how to sword fight.

QUEEN
What do you mean, "he"?

MAGIC MIRROR
Unfortunately, as the years passed, there was no baby and they began to despair.

KING, QUEEN, ARTISTS
SIGH!

MAGIC MIRROR
Finally, in her desperation, the Queen turned to the one person she knew could give her the answers she sought. The most intelligent and articulate being in all the kingdom...me.

QUEEN approaches MAGIC MIRROR

QUEEN
Oh Magic Mirror on the Wall, who sees all things and knows it all, will I have a babe to have and hold, before I'm gray and grow too old?

MAGIC MIRROR
I'm glad you asked my Queen, though you didn't have to rhyme.

QUEEN
Oh really? I thought it was customary.

MAGIC MIRROR
Only in fairy tales my Queen. This is real life.
    (Winks at audience.)
Prose is fine. To answer your question though, yes. You will have a baby!

KING, QUEEN and ARTISTS celebrate.

KING and QUEEN
We're going to have a baby! We're going to have a baby!

QUEEN
Tell us Mirror, will it be a boy or a girl?

MAGIC MIRROR
Yes.

KING and QUEEN look at EACH OTHER, then MAGIC MIRROR.

KING and QUEEN
WHICH ONE???

MAGIC MIRROR
A girl.

QUEEN
(Ecstatic.)
A girl!

KING
(Not as ecstatic.)
A girl?

QUEEN
She will learn to sing and dance and paint and sculpt and act and…

KING
Sword fight?

QUEEN
Sword fight?

KING
I was really hoping I'd get to teach someone to sword fight.

MAGIC MIRROR
And so you shall.

KING
What do you mean, Mirror?

MAGIC MIRROR
Yes indeed. She must learn all about the Arts, including the art of sword fighting. It will figure very prominently in her destiny.

KING, QUEEN, ARTISTS
Oooooooooooo…..

QUEEN
Her destiny?

MAGIC MIRROR
Destiny. Noun. Something that is to happen in the future.
> (Small pause.)

So…one day, as I had predicted, the little princess was born.

> THE STORK enters, wearing a delivery uniform, carrying a bundle and clipboard.

MAGIC MIRROR
Who are you supposed to be?

STORK
I'm the Stork. What's the matter? Don't you know where babies come from?
> (Hands clipboard to KING.)

Sign here, please.
> (KING signs, hands clipboard back as STORK hands bundle to QUEEN. STORK exits.)

KING
> (Looking at baby.)

She's so beautiful! What shall we name her, my dear?

QUEEN
Let's name her after your mother.

KING
Aurora Borealis? That's an awful name.

MAGIC MIRROR
How about just Aurora?

QUEEN
Aurora? That's nice. I like that.

KING
Any chance we'll face litigation over that name from a certain "mouse-eared" company?

MAGIC MIRROR
Litigation. Noun. A lawsuit brought about in a court of law.

KING
So what you're saying is...?

MAGIC MIRROR
It's entirely possible.

KING
Oh well...Aurora it is!

> THE KING plays with the baby.

KING
Coochie, coochie, coo!

MAGIC MIRROR
And so...the King and Queen had a large celebration in honor of the young princess' arrival. Everyone in the kingdom was invited. Including the magic folk or Fairies as you might call them.

> MUSIC: Festive party music. THE 3 FAIRIES enter and stand before the KING and QUEEN.

MAGIC MIRROR
The first fairy to step forward and offer her gift was Melody.

MELODY steps forward.

MELODY
Little princess, I bestow upon you the gift of music, so that all of your days will be filled with the joy and happiness that song brings.

SHE steps back.

MAGIC MIRROR
Next was Arabesque.

ARABESQUE steps forward.

ARABESQUE
Little one, I bestow upon you the gift of dance. May your movements be rhythmic and your steps be ever true.

SHE steps back.

MAGIC MIRROR
And finally, Thesbe stepped forward.
(THESBE steps forward.)
But just as she was about to bestow her gift, there was a flash of lightning and a crash of thunder!

LIGHTS: Flash. SOUND: Thunder. EVIL FAIRY enters, strikes a pose. EVERYONE cowers.

MAGIC MIRROR
She's magnificent!

EVIL FAIRY
Or something like that.
(Looks around.)
Well, well, well. What a nice party. Music. Dancing. Cake. Gifts. In fact, I see everything one could possibly want at a party, the only thing missing…IS ME!!!
(Yelling.)
WHY WASN'T I INVITED TO THIS PARTY???

THE KING and QUEEN look at EACH OTHER.

KING
I was under the impression we had invited everyone in the kingdom. Isn't that what I said? Let's make sure we invite everyone in the kingdom?

QUEEN
We did invite everyone in the kingdom! I made the invitations myself!

KING
Perhaps the invitation got lost in the mail?

EVERYONE looks at the STORK.

STORK
(Gulps.)
It's entirely possible.

EVIL FAIRY
I will not suffer this indignation lightly! I will have my revenge!

SHE steps toward the baby.

KING and QUEEN
NO!!!

EVIL FAIRY

Here is my gift!
(Raises HER arms.)
ON HER 16^(TH) BIRTHDAY, THE LITTLE PRINCESS SHALL PRICK HER FINGER UPON THE SPINDLE OF A SPINNING WHEEL AND DIE!!! BWAH-HA-HA-HA-HA!!!

> LIGHTS: Flash. SOUND: Thunder.

ALL

GASP!!!

MAGIC MIRROR

Wow. Isn't that a bit harsh? After all, this is Children's Theatre.

EVIL FAIRY

Let this be a lesson to each and every one of you! If you're going to invite me to your party, you better get delivery confirmation! Bwah-ha-ha-ha-ha!!!

> SHE exits laughing. EVERYONE looks at EACH OTHER.

QUEEN
(To KING.)
What are we to do?

KING

I don't know, my darling.

> THESBE steps forward.

THESBE

Perhaps I can help.

KING

Thesbe?

THESBE
I have not yet given my gift.

QUEEN
Thesbe? Can you reverse this curse?

THESBE
Alas, no. What has been done cannot be undone...not completely...but, I may be able to soften the curse...may I?

> THESBE gestures for the baby. The QUEEN hands the bundle to HER.

THESBE
I proclaim that the princess will not die when the spindle pricks her finger but instead will fall into a deep sleep. A sleep from which she will awaken in a thousand years with the kiss of a hero.

> Pause.

KING
A thousand years? That's your idea of softening the curse?

THESBE
It's the best I could do.

QUEEN
Yes. It IS better than death! Much better than that! Thank you, Thesbe!

KING
As King, I can do my part to prevent this curse as well! I hereby decree that all spinning wheels in this kingdom will be immediately and thoroughly smashed into a million pieces! Now everybody go and destroy those spinning wheels!

> The CROWD goes crazy, running off in

> every direction as we hear the sounds of
> destruction. CAST MEMBERS may cross
> stage with axes and sledge hammers, pieces
> of spinning wheels. SOUND: Crashing and
> smashing.

MAGIC MIRROR
> (Alone on stage.)

Pandemonium. Noun. Chaos. Confusion. Disorder.
> (Pause.)

For the next 16 years, the King and Queen, along with help from the Fairies and all of the kingdom's artists raised the young princess to be not only an incredible singer, dancer, actor and painter but also a formidable sword fighter!

> MUSIC: Adventurous music plays as we see
> various scenes of people entering with the
> bundle, dancing, painting, sword fighting,
> etc Then transitioning into scenes with
> AURORA, doing the same activities as SHE
> grows older. Finally, the MUSIC: fades.

MAGIC MIRROR

Schtick. Yiddish word. Comedic business. Finally, the big day came. Princess Aurora's 16th birthday! The palace was very quiet. Everyone remained in their rooms afraid to come out. Afraid that somehow, despite their best efforts, the Evil Fairy's curse would come to pass.

> SOUND: Doorbell. Long pause. SOUND:
> Doorbell. Long pause. Finally, the STORK
> enters, pushing a large wrapped package,
> obviously in the shape of a spinning wheel.

STORK

Geez! Where is everybody?
> (Calls out.)

Hello? Is anybody home?
> (HE looks at clipboard.)

I have a birthday gift here for the princess from…
> (Looks at clipboard again.)

Millie…no…Melasone…Malignant…Minnie Mouse…oh never mind. I'll just leave it right here. Somebody'll know just what to do with it.

> HE exits.

MAGIC MIRROR

And then, this happened.

> AURORA enters.

AURORA
> (Singing.)

Happy Birthday to me. Happy Birthday to me…
> (Looks around.)

Hello? Where is everybody?
> (Addresses audience.)

You think they forgot what today is?
> (Notices gift.)

Well! It looks like someone remembered!
> (Tears paper and bow off.)

What is this thing? I've never seen anything like it. It has a wheel but it's not a carriage. I wonder what it does?
> (SHE runs HER hand over it.)

Ouch! I pricked my finger! That's odd. All of a sudden I feel…

> SHE falls over and doesn't move.

MAGIC MIRROR
Once upon a time, a beautiful princess was placed under a magic spell by an evil fairy. A spell that would cause her to fall into a deep, deep sleep. A sleep from which she would awaken a thousand years later.

> LIGHTS: Fade as MUSIC: Futuristic music plays. LIGHTS: Rise on palace, now covered with vines and trees. The MAGIC MIRROR sits empty. At center sits a bed, also overgrown with vines. SOUND: A battle is heard in the distance, voices, even lasers and heavy equipment if possible.

BUCK
(Offstage.)
This way! There's some kind of old building back here!

> BUCK enters, looking around. HE is a heroic spaceman and carries a ray gun. HE is followed by MR. ROBOTO, a robot, played by the MAGIC MIRROR and STORK, now dressed in black. ALL carry ray guns.

STORK
What is this place?

BUCK
Some ancient palace from the looks of it.

MR. ROBOTO
Biddi-biddi-biddi. VERY ancient.

BUCK
Did the zombies see you enter?

STORK
No, I don't believe they did.

>   HE examines the bed.

                    BUCK
Good. We'll lay low for a bit, see what happens.

                    STORK
Commander! Look at this!

>   He pulls some of the vines from the bed,
>   revealing AURORA.

                    MR. ROBOTO
Hubba-hubba-hubba! What a babe!

>   THEY uncover HER.

                    BUCK
She's alive...but apparently in some sort of stasis!

                    MR. ROBOTO
Biddi-biddi-biddi. Stasis. Noun. A state or condition in which things do not change, move, or progress.

                    STORK
                    (To BUCK.)
Does he always have to do that?

                    BUCK
It's part of his programming.

                    MR. ROBOTO
Old habits are hard to break.
                    (Winks at audience.)
Biddi-biddi-biddi.

                    BUCK
I wonder how long she's been here?

STORK
A very long time from the looks of it.

MR. ROBOTO
Offhand I'd say she's been here a thousand years. Biddi-biddi-biddi.

BUCK
A thousand years? How is that possible?

MR. ROBOTO
There is an ancient legend, Buck. A young princess was cursed to sleep a thousand years by the Evil Fairy.

STORK
Wait...I know of this story. It is one that my people tell to our young. A cautionary tale intended to warn them of crossing the Evil One. You mean to tell me that it's real? That this is the Sleeping Beauty?

MR. ROBOTO
Biddi-biddi-biddi. Yep.

BUCK
Does the legend say anything about waking her up?

STORK
Yes...as I recall, at the end of her thousand year slumber she will be awakened by the kiss of a true hero.

> ALL of THEM look at audience, check THEIR breath, look at EACH other.

BUCK
We can't all kiss her.

STORK
Agreed. I should do it.

BUCK
Why you?

STORK
I am the Stork. The greatest warrior the Stork people have ever known.

BUCK
You're the only Stork person left!

STORK
How dare you! You had to bring that up, didn't you? To remind me that I am the very last survivor of a once proud and thriving race of Ciconiidae. (AUTHOR NOTE: Sic-con-KNEE-a-dee.) Now, nearly extinct!
(HE does a weird bird call.)

MR. ROBOTO
Biddi-biddi-biddi.

BUCK
There's only one way to solve this dilemma.

BUCK, STORK, MR. ROBOTO
ROCK, PAPER, RAY GUNS!

BUCK
It's the only way.

MR. ROBOTO
Biddi-biddi-biddi.

BUCK
See, even Mr. Roboto agrees.

STORK
He's programmed to agree with everything you say.

                    MR. ROBOTO
Biddi-biddi-biddi.

                    BUCK
Thanks Mr. Roboto.

                    MR. ROBOTO
Biddi-biddi-biddi. Whatever you say, Buck.

                    BUCK
Ok. Here we go.

                              THEY play. ALL choose ray guns. THEY
                              do it again. ALL choose ray guns.

                    STORK
This is ridiculous. We can't all choose ray guns every time.

                              THEY do it again. ALL choose ray guns.

                    BUCK
Look, I have an idea. Let's try it again and this time we'll all close our eyes, all right?

                    STORK
Fine.

                    MR. ROBOTO
Biddi-biddi-biddi.

                    BUCK
Ok. Everyone close your eyes…or ocular devices as it were. And…

                              HE steps to the bed, as THEY play and
                              kisses AURORA. THEY open THEIR eyes
                              and realize THEY have been tricked.

STORK, MR. ROBOTO

Hey!

AURORA sits up suddenly.

AURORA

…really, really sleepy.
(Looks around, confused.)
Who are you?

BUCK

You were right Stork! The kiss worked!

AURORA

Right about what? What kiss? Who are you guys?

BUCK

I am Rebel Commander Phillip Rogers, but my friends call me Buck. This is my team, the Stork and Mr. Roboto.

STORK

Greetings.

MR. ROBOTO

Biddi-biddi-biddi. You're hot.

AURORA jumps out of bed.

AURORA

What rebellion are you commander of? Where am I?

BUCK

Take it easy…

AURORA

Aurora. Princess Aurora! And I command you to tell me what's going on!

BUCK

You are on the planet Earth, Princess, or at least what remains of it. Once the second most populated planet in the star system of Sol.

> AURORA notices the condition of the palace for the first time.

AURORA

What has become of the palace...this is my home...where is my family? The King and Queen?

BUCK

Princess. No one has lived in this place for...hundreds of years.

AURORA

Hundreds...?
> (Long pause, looking around at the ruins of her home. Realizing.)

The Evil Fairy! She did this didn't she?

MR. ROBOTO

Biddi-biddi-biddi. Oh snap!

BUCK

The Evil Fairy rules the entire universe, Princess. She has ruled with an iron fist for centuries.

AURORA

Centuries? What year is this?

STORK

It's 2472, your Highness.

AURORA

2472? You mean I've been asleep for a thousand years?

STORK
Yes. I suppose you have.

MR. ROBOTO
Biddi-biddi-biddi. You look really good for a woman your age!

SPACE ZOMBIES enter, growling.

BUCK
Oh no! They've found us!

AURORA
What are they?

BUCK
Space Zombies!

AURORA
Space Zombies?

BUCK, STORK, MR. ROBOTO
SPACE ZOMBIES!!!

MR. ROBOTO
Biddi-biddi-biddi.

BUCK
Stay behind us, Princess. We'll protect you!

AURORA
I don't think so!

SHE grabs HER sword from beside the bed and leads the attack. Together, THEY run the SPACE ZOMBIES off.

BUCK
Where did you learn to fight like that?

AURORA
My father taught me.

BUCK
Wise man.

AURORA
Wise king. And if you think my sword fighting skills are impressive you should see me dance.

BUCK
Dance? What's that?

AURORA
You don't know what dancing is?

BUCK looks at STORK.

BUCK
Mr. Roboto? Can you help us?

MR. ROBOTO
Searching… Searching…Dance. Verb. To move rhythmically to music, typically following a set sequence of steps…an archaic form of expression believed to have been outlawed by the Evil Fairy along with all other forms of art in the mid 21st Century.

AURORA
Outlawed? You mean you have no art at all? No music? No poetry?

BUCK
No.

AURORA
How do you express yourselves? How do you show joy? Or sadness? Or love? If you have no art or music?

Pause.

          BUCK
What is…music?

          Everyone turns to MR. ROBOTO.

          MR. ROBOTO
Searching…Ah yes…that'll do nicely.

          MUSIC: Slow song plays. AURORA turns to face BUCK.

          AURORA
May I have this dance?

          BUCK
But, I don't know how.

          AURORA
Just listen to the music and follow me.

          THEY dance, slowly as the LIGHTS: Fade MUSIC: Continues into the BLACKOUT. LIGHTS: Rise, we see a harsh wasteland. The wreckage of what was once a great city. THREE RAGGED FIGURES are huddled over a barrel fire for warmth. THEY are cloaked such that we cannot see THEIR faces. THE EVIL FAIRY enters.

          EVIL FAIRY
Be gone with you!

          THE RAGGED FIGURES scatter and crouch nearby. SPACE ZOMBIES enter.

          EVIL FAIRY
It's about time! Did you capture Rebel Commander Rogers?

SPACE ZOMBIE #1

Rrurrgh!

EVIL FAIRY

You let him get away?

SPACE ZOMBIE #2

Rrurrgh!

EVIL FAIRY

I wasn't talking to you, now was I?

SPACE ZOMBIE #2

Rrurrgh!

EVIL FAIRY

Well, you should be!

SPACE ZOMBIE #1

Rrurrgh!

EVIL FAIRY

So, you did find Rogers!

ALL SPACE ZOMBIES

Rrurrgh!

EVIL FAIRY

Would everyone stop trying to talk at once!

Pause.

SPACE ZOMBIE #1

Rrurrgh!

EVIL FAIRY

I see. And then what happened?

SPACE ZOMBIE #1

Rrurrgh!

EVIL FAIRY

What? Can this be true?

SHE looks at the SPACE ZOMBIES. THEY all nod "yes".

SPACE ZOMBIE #1

Rrurrgh!

EVIL FAIRY

A girl?

SPACE ZOMBIE #1

Rrurrgh!

EVIL FAIRY

With a sword? Interesting. Hmmm…what year is this?

SPACE ZOMBIE #2

Rrurrgh!

EVIL FAIRY

2472? Really? I've been so busy conquering the universe that I've lost track of time. I'm really going to have to buy a date book… anyway…it's true! Sleeping Beauty has awakened from her slumber! No matter though! I'll take my entire army of Space Zombies and wipe out Commander Rogers and his Rebels and finish the job I started a thousand years ago! I hope you've enjoyed your time here in the future Princess, because your stay is going to be very short! Bwah-ha-ha-ha-ha! Space Zombies! Prepare for a full scale attack!!!

ALL SPACE ZOMBIES

RRURRGH!!!

> EVIL FAIRY and SPACE ZOMBIES exit, screaming. The THREE RAGGED FIGURES cross to center.

RAGGED FIGURE #1

We must hurry Sisters. We may be able to warn Aurora of the Evil Fairy's attack!

> THEY exit. LIGHTS: Blackout as dark music plays into scene change. LIGHTS: Rise on Palace. The vines have been removed now as has the bed. BUCK, STORK and ROBOTO enter.

BUCK

This palace will serve as the new headquarters for the Rebel Forces. If we are to make a final stand against the Space Zombies, this is as fine a place as any and Princess Aurora has agreed to let us use it.

STORK

Where is the Princess, anyway?

BUCK

Changing clothes. But here she comes. May I present the newest member of the rebellion...the Sleeping Beauty herself!

> AURORA enters wearing spacesuit.

MR. ROBOTO

Biddi-biddi-biddi. Wowsers!

AURORA

Thank you, Mr. Roboto. You know what they say. When in Rome.

STORK

What's Rome?

MR. ROBOTO
Searching...

RAGGED FIGURES
(Offstage.)
Aurora!

> THEY pull THEIR weapons as the THREE RAGGED FIGURES enter.

STORK
Who are they?

BUCK
They don't look like Space Zombies!

AURORA
How do you know my name?

RAGGED FIGURE #1
We know your name, Princess...because we were there on the day you received it.

RAGGED FIGURE #2
The day we bestowed great gifts upon you.

RAGGED FIGURE #3
And now you must use those gifts.

AURORA
Wait...could it be?

RAGGED FIGURE #1
Yes, Aurora. It is us.

> The RAGGED FIGURES remove THEIR hoods to reveal MELODY, ARABESQUE and THESBE.

AURORA
Melody! Arabesque! Thesbe! You're here? You're still alive?

ARABESQUE
We are Fairies dear, we're immortal.

BUCK, STORK, MR. ROBOTO
(Raising THEIR ray guns.)
FAIRIES???

AURORA
No! Wait! Put your ray guns away! These are good Fairies.

BUCK
(Lowering ray gun.)
Good Fairies? I didn't know such a thing existed.

THESBE
Certainly we exist but the Evil Fairy has kept us powerless for centuries.

AURORA
How?

MELODY
Our power has always come from the Arts, Aurora. Music and dance and theatre and poetry. The Evil Fairy had removed these things from the world for so long but when you woke up you began immediately to return them to the world... to return our power to us once more. But we must warn you Princess, she will not stand for this! She is on her way here now with her army to destroy you.

BUCK
On her way now?

SPACE ZOMBIES enter on all sides.

ARABESQUE
You can defeat this army Aurora. Only you.

AURORA
Me? But how?

THESBE
Your gifts!

MELODY, ARABESQUE, THESBE
Use your gifts, Aurora.

> AURORA looks around at EVERYONE.
> The SPACE ZOMBIES close in.

AURORA
Hit it Mr. Roboto!

> MUSIC: Something spectacular and fun.
> AURORA begins to dance. SHE is joined
> by the FAIRIES then BUCK, STORK and
> MR. ROBOTO. Finally, the SPACE
> ZOMBIES join in as well. When the dance
> has ended, ALL cheer.

SPACE ZOMBIE #1
Rrurrgh!

AURORA
What did he say?

MR. ROBOTO
Biddi-biddi-biddi. He said thank you. For teaching them how to dance.

SPACE ZOMBIE #2
Rrurrgh!

AURORA
And what did he say?

MR. ROBOTO
Biddi-biddi-biddi. HE said the Evil Fairy is gonna be pretty ticked off when she finds out about this!

EVIL FAIRY
(From offstage.)
He's right about that!

STORK
Look! It's the Evil Fairy!

BUCK
And she's turned into a dragon!

> The SPACE ZOMBIES run off screaming. MUSIC: Battle music. The EVIL FAIRY enters as a dragon. BUCK comes to AURORA'S side.

EVIL FAIRY
Back off Buck Rogers! This is between me and Sleeping Beauty!!!

> SHE knocks BUCK out of the way. AURORA battles the EVIL FAIRY. The battle takes place all over the palace. Finally, AURORA gains the upper hand and is about to strike the final blow, but hesitates.

EVIL FAIRY
What are you waiting for? Finish the job!

AURORA
No.

EVERYONE looks around.

EVIL FAIRY

No?

AURORA

No. A great disservice was done to you once upon a time and although I was only an infant when it happened, it was YOUR reaction to that slight that was childish. I spare you your life this day in the hope that you will see the error of your ways... But understand this... your reign has ended. From this day forward we will bring music and dance and poetry and theatre and art back to this world!

EVERYONE cheers. The EVIL FAIRY exits, defeated.

AURORA
(To CAST and audience.)
My parents, the King and Queen, loved the Arts and they in turn, taught me to love the Arts. In fact, there was once, long ago, a tradition in my kingdom. At the end of an adventure we would have a grand celebration, where everyone in the kingdom would get down with their bad selves!
(To MR. ROBOTO.)
Mr. Roboto?

MR. ROBOTO
Biddi-biddi-biddi. Let's boogie!!!

MUSIC: Something loud and fun.
EVERYONE dances.

THE END

Snow White
and the
~~Seven~~ 47 Dwarves

A PLAY
FOR YOUNG AUDIENCES

BY

L. HENRY DOWELL

BLACK BOX THEATRE PUBLISHING

CAST

Snow White
The Magic Mirror
The Evil Queen
The Huntsman
Prince
7 Dwarves
Council of the 47 Dwarves
Fuzzy Forest Creatures

The Divas
Cinderella, Sleeping Beauty, The Little Mermaid,
Repunzel, Princess Jasmine, Belle, Pocahontas

The Villains
Cruella, The Mad Hatter,
The Big Bad Wolf's Cousin Earl,
The Wicked Witch, Captain Hook, The Boogey Man,
Tweedle Dee and Tweedle Dum.

In the script the Seven Dwarves are numbered #1 - #7. They have purposely NOT been named. At the beginning of the play the audience may be pooled in order to name the Dwarves. The actors must then act their parts based on the names that the audience has selected for them. In past productions a list of possible names was chosen through the rehearsal process and printed in the program. Some of those names which were quite effective and funny were:

Stinky	Baby	Farmer	Elvis
Moody	Nerdy	Doctor	Pirate
Macho	Nose Picker	Hippie	Janitor
Itchy	Flirty	Old	Insensitive
Shakespeare	Brainy	French	Crossdresser
Cheerleader	Cowboy	Tourist	Nervous
Overactive Bladder	Hillbilly	Secret Agent	Robot
Director	Gangster	Sgt. Dwarf	Ninja

These names are only suggestions. Feel free to discover other possibilities. The lines remain the same; it's the way they are played which provides the comedy in the Dwarves' scenes. It is advisable to have a selection of props and hats backstage that might be used in connection with the names that are picked by the audience. Casts should be discouraged, however, from improvising lines during the performance. If played by a talented cast, this show has proven to be one that audiences return to for multiple performances.

The Council of the 47 Dwarves can contain as many or as few Dwarves as you have. Likewise for the Fuzzy Forest Creatures which can contain any animals you want. The roles in the script, Cat, Skunk, Deer, etc. are only suggestions.

Above all, the roles in this play should be played with maximum Gusto! Theatre should always be fun!

The action of this play is continuous. When a scene ends on one part of the stage, the lights blackout, but immediately rise on another part of the stage. If your production requires time between scenes, scene change music may be used in addition to the suggested music styles in the play.

SNOW WHITE AND THE 47 DWARVES

SETTING: The pre-show lights illuminate the stage. On stage right there is a castle wall with a large mirror hanging from it. The back of the stage contains a forest, and on stage left a small cottage of THE DWARVES with a table and several small chairs. THE SEVEN DWARVES enter and the audience chooses seven names for THEM from a list. This process can be handled by a cast member, or Director. Throughout the play THEY will play THEIR characters based on those names. When THEY exit, the play begins. There is SPOOKY MUSIC. LIGHTS rise on THE MAGIC MIRROR, whose face now appears in the mirror on the wall.

MIRROR
Good evening everyone. I am the Magic Mirror on the wall, and I'm here to tell you the story of Snow White and the Forty-seven Dwarves. Now, first let me assure you that word is pronounced "Dwarves" with a "v" and not "Dwarfs" with an "f" as you may have seen elsewhere. You see, we mirrors are very knowledgeable about these sort of things. And now for our story...
    (Clears throat, comically.)
One snowy night in a castle far, far away, a little princess was born.
    (SOUND: A loud, crying baby is heard.)
Her parents named her Snow White. As the years passed, the child grew up to be a lovely young woman. Her beauty and her gentle nature won the hearts of all who knew her. But of all her attributes, the greatest was her lovely singing voice.

    SNOW WHITE enters in potato sack,
    singing a Motown tune.

MIRROR
You go, girlfriend!

SNOW WHITE
Thank you very much.

MIRROR
No. I mean you go…offstage now.

SNOW WHITE
Oh.

> SHE exits.

MIRROR
After Snow White's father died, she lived in the castle with her stepmother, the Evil Queen.

> QUEEN enters, dressed in black, and strikes a pose.

MIRROR
As you can see, the Queen was very beautiful, but she was also cold and heartless.

QUEEN
I heard that!

MIRROR
It's true. The mirror doesn't lie. She was also extremely jealous of Snow White's beauty.

QUEEN
I am not!

MIRROR
Are too!

QUEEN

Am not!

MIRROR

Are too!

QUEEN

Am not!

MIRROR
She was also a little childish.

QUEEN
Just get on with it!

MIRROR
On Tuesday nights, the Evil Queen would teach a class in Villainy 101. Her students included some of the vilest and most despicable villains the world had ever seen. Cruella!

CRUELLA enters.

CRUELLA
Puppies! Puppies! I hate puppies! Is that a puppy? Puppies!!!

MIRROR
The Mad Hatter!

HE enters laughing

MIRROR
Tweedle Dee and Tweedle Dum

THEY enter.
TWEEDLE DUM
Hey! Who you calling dum?

TWEEDLE DEE
You, ya big dummy!

TWEEDLE DUM

Take that back!

TWEEDLE DEE

Make me!

TWEEDLE DUM

Shut up!

TWEEDLE DEE

You shut up!

MIRROR

Both of you shut up!

BOTH

Ok.

MIRROR

The Wicked Witch of the West!

SHE enters, laughing.

MIRROR

Captain Hook!

HOOK enters.

HOOK

Hey kids! Wanna hear a joke? Why wouldn't the little boy's mother let him watch the Pirate movie? Because it was rated AARR! Get it? You know what a Pirate's favorite type of sweater is? AARR-gyle! You know what a Pirate's favorite restaurant is?

MIRROR

Let me guess, is it AARR-bys?

HOOK
Nope. Long John Silvers.

MIRROR
Moving right along...The Boogey Man!

HE enters.

BOOGEY MAN
Hey Baby! What's shakin'? Slap me some skin Cap'n Hook!

HOOK high fives HIM with HIS hook.

BOOGEY MAN
Hey! Is that a cockroach on the floor there?
(Picks it up and eats it.)
Yum! Yum! I love cockroaches!

WICKED WITCH
That's disgusting!

HOOK
You're telling me.

CRUELLA
Puppies.

MAD HATTER
Enough with the puppies already!

CRUELLA
But I love them!

MAD HATTER
I thought you hated them.

CRUELLA
I do. I do.

TWEEDLE DEE
She's obsessed.

TWEEDLE DUM
No doubt. EMO.

TWEEDLE DEE
Yep.

CRUELLA
I AM NOT EMO!!!

MIRROR
...and last, but not least...the Big Bad Wolf!

> WOLF enters wearing flannel and a John Deere hat.

WOLF
Howdy y'all.

> THEY look at EACH OTHER.

MIRROR
Wait a minute, you aren't the Big Bad Wolf.

WOLF
Nah, I'm his cousin Earl.

MIRROR
Where's the Big Bad Wolf?

WOLF
He had traffic school. I'm fillin' in for him.

MIRROR
Oh...ok then...anyway, on Tuesday nights the Evil Queen would teach this cadre of villains the finer points of... villainy.

QUEEN enters.

QUEEN

Tonight's topic of discussion will be a villain's laugh. You see, the way a villain laughs defines him...or her. The moment that he laughs his laugh, all the good guys must despise him...or her. Now, I want to hear each one of you laugh.

EACH ONE takes a turn.

QUEEN

Pitiful. Now listen. This is how a true villain laughs. Bwah-ha-ha-ha-ha! Now repeat after me. Bwah-ha-ha-ha-ha!

VILLAINS

Bwah-ha-ha-ha-ha!

QUEEN

Bwah-ha-ha-ha-ha!

VILLAINS

Bwah-ha-ha-ha-ha!

QUEEN

You know, there just might be some hope for you miserable curs after all!

LIGHTS: BLACKOUT, then RISE on MIRROR.

MIRROR

Bwah-ha-ha-ha-ha...oh, never mind. Anyway, the Queen dressed the Princess in rags and forced her to clean the entire castle like a maid.

SNOW WHITE enters dressed in a potato sack. SHE carries a bucket and wears rubber gloves. SHE scrubs the floor. SHE works hard and sings "Swing Low, Sweet Chariot". THE QUEEN enters and inspects the job.

QUEEN
You missed a spot.

MIRROR
Despite the back breaking work and rough treatment, Snow White never lost her sunny disposition.

SNOW WHITE
I did miss a spot! How nice of you to point that out, Evil Stepmother.

QUEEN exits.

MIRROR
Sometimes Snow White would be visited by all of the Princesses in the neighboring kingdoms. They would sit around discussing issues of great importance.

PRINCESSES enter.

CINDERELLA
...and did you see what she wore to the ball? I mean, what century does she think this is anyway? Oh, Snow White, you missed a spot, dear.

SNOW WHITE
Thanks, Cinderella.

BELLE
Oh, Cinderella, you pay far too much attention to things like that.

PRINCESS JASMINE
I agree with you totally, Belle.

BELLE
Thank you, Princess Jasmine.

REPUNZEL
Me too.

THE LITTLE MERMAID
Absolutely.

CINDERELLA
And how about you, Sleeping Beauty?

SHE is snoring, leaning against the wall.

CINDERELLA
Or maybe we should call her "Snoring" Beauty!

THEY giggle. POCAHONTAS nudges HER.

SLEEPING BEAUTY
(Waking suddenly.)
I didn't do it! I don't know how that got there officer! Hey...did I miss something?

CINDERELLA
Try and stay awake dear.

SLEEPING BEAUTY
Sorry.

BELLE
Like I was saying, I think it's what's on the inside that counts.

THEY laugh, except POCAHONTAS.

POCAHONTAS
Girls...we shouldn't laugh at Belle. She's right. It doesn't matter what a person looks like on the outside.

CINDERELLA
Says the girl wearing the buckskin! Who helped you make that outfit, Pocahontas? Your grandma?

POCAHONTAS
Actually, yes...so what?

CINDERELLA
Oh, don't be so sensitive. Here's some rocks...now amuse yourself.
(Hands HER rocks.)

POCAHONTAS
Oooooooo.......rocks.

SHE sits and plays with them.

CINDERELLA
So, is there any new news to report? Snow White? Have you found a boyfriend yet?

SNOW WHITE
(Shyly.)
No. Not yet.

REPUNZEL
Maybe if you grew your hair longer? Guys seem to like that.

BELLE
Maybe you should lower your standards slightly.

THEY look at HER.

BELLE
Well, it worked for me.

CINDERELLA
Yes, we've all seen that "Beast" you're dating.

REPUNZEL
What are you waiting for dear, Prince Charming to come riding along on a white horse?

CINDERELLA
Please. We've all been down that road before.

SLEEPING BEAUTY
Yes, Prince Charming does get around, doesn't he?

> ALL giggle, then look at EACH OTHER suspiciously.

PRINCESS JASMINE
Maybe I could ask the Genie to help find you a boyfriend.

> THEY giggle again.

BELLE
Girls, we shouldn't tease poor Snow White. She has a hard enough time as it is.

CINDERELLA
Oh, Belle, must you be so...Pollyanna-ish?

BELLE
Must you be such a Diva?

GIRLS
GASP!

CINDERELLA
Now Belle...being a Diva is more than just an attitude. It's a way of life. Wake up, Sleeping Beauty!

SLEEPING BEAUTY
I'm awake! I'm awake! Where are we? What's going on?

CINDERELLA
I was just explaining to our friend, Snow White, what it means to be a Diva.

SLEEPING BEAUTY
Oooooo......I love being a Diva!

CINDERELLA
Girls! Assume Diva poses!

> THEY do. Primping and fluffing THEIR hair.

CINDERELLA
Just like the old song says, it's all about R-E-S-P-E-C-T.

POCAHONTAS
That spells respect.

CINDERELLA
Yes. Very good, Pocahontas.

REPUNZEL
It's about attitude.

PRINCESS JASMINE
And keeping things positive.

SLEEPING BEAUTY
Don't let anyone push you around.

BELLE
Or get you down.

LITTLE MERMAID
Just be yourself. I had to learn that lesson the hard way.

CINDERELLA
You got that, Snow White?

SNOW WHITE
Got it. I think.

CINDERELLA
Good. Now, come on girls. Let's go to the mall!

PRINCESSES
The mall!

> THEY exit, except for SLEEPING
> BEAUTY, who has fallen asleep.
> POCAHONTAS re-enters and taps HER on
> the shoulder, waking HER. THEY exit.
> LIGHTS OUT except on MIRROR.

MIRROR
Never a dull moment around here. Anyway, the Queen's most prized possession was her gorgeous, antique, magic mirror…let me tell you, it was beautiful, with a hand carved frame and a…

QUEEN
(Entering.)
Ok, ok, we get it.

MIRROR
Every day the Queen would stand in front of her mirror…well, in front of me, and ask a question…

QUEEN
Magic Mirror on the wall, who's the fairest one of all?

MIRROR
And every day, the mirror, who was very articulate, would reply…
"You O' Queen are the fairest in the land."

> QUEEN
> (To audience.)

Darn tootin!

> SHE exits.

> MIRROR

While the Queen spent the majority of her time admiring herself, poor little Snow White had to work long hours in the castle, often singing and dancing while she worked.

> DANCE MUSIC begins. SNOW WHITE enters, dancing with a broom. SHE exits and re-enters with a feather duster. SHE exits then re-enters with a toilet plunger. MUSIC ends.

> MIRROR

One day, while Snow White was…plunging the toilet, she made a special wish.

> SNOW WHITE

Oh, how I wish with all my heart that a handsome Prince would come along and carry me away!

> MIRROR

No sooner had Snow White uttered those words, than a handsome "Prince" appeared!

> PRINCE MUSIC. A purple light illuminates PRINCE. HE wears all purple with high heels. HE dances as the MUSIC blares. HE dances around HER. MUSIC ends.

> PRINCE

Hey Baby.

> SNOW WHITE

Why, hello there.

PRINCE
You sure are pretty. I dig tall chicks.

SNOW WHITE
Thank you…uh….Prince.

PRINCE
Nice weather we're having, huh?

SNOW WHITE
Looks like rain to me.

PRINCE
I like rain. Especially "Purple Rain".

SNOW WHITE
Purple rain? Where'd you see that? That sounds crazy. Was it because of pollution?

MIRROR
Although Prince was an interesting character, Snow White was very shy.

SNOW WHITE
I'm very shy.

PRINCE
I can dig that.

SNOW WHITE
Have we met before?

PRINCE
I don't think so.

SNOW WHITE
You seem very familiar to me.

PRINCE
Of course I do. Everyone knows me. I'm Prince. And, by the way, I brought you a present.

SNOW WHITE
A present! What is it?

PRINCE
Well, a present is a gift you give to someone, but that really isn't important right now. Here.

> Hands HER a box. SHE opens it.

SNOW WHITE
Wow....it's a...purple hat.

PRINCE
It's not just a purple hat. It's a raspberry beret. The kind you find in a second hand store.

SNOW WHITE
Wow. Thanks big spender. I'll treasure it always.
    (Throws it into audience.)

MIRROR
The Prince was quite smitten with Snow White.

PRINCE
I am quite smitten with you.

MIRROR
Snow White on the other hand was troubled by the feeling that somehow she knew Prince from somewhere else.

SNOW WHITE
Hey, look over there! It's something purple!

PRINCE
Something purple?! Where?

SHE runs away.

PRINCE
(To audience.)
I love it when they play hard to get.

HE exits.

MIRROR
That evening, as usual, the Evil Queen stood before her Magic Mirror.

QUEEN enters.

QUEEN
Magic Mirror on the wall, who's the fairest one of all?

MIRROR
Well Queen, you see…

QUEEN
Mirror?

MIRROR
It's kind of like this…

QUEEN
Tell me!

MIRROR
Are you sure you really want to know?

QUEEN
Of course I do. Why would I have asked you unless I wanted to know?

MIRROR
You may not like the answer O' Queen!

QUEEN
What? Really?

MIRROR
Well…

QUEEN
(Extremely mad. Yelling.)
Tell me! I command you!

MIRROR
As you wish.
(Clears throat.)
"Her lips blood red. Her hair like night. Her skin like snow. Her name…Snow White!"

QUEEN
(Flipping her lid.)
SAY WHAT??? How can this be? She's so…cheerful and…
(Looks for another word, but can't think of one.)
Cheerful! Mirror, do you really think she's more beautiful than me?

MIRROR
I calls 'em like I sees 'em.

QUEEN stomps back and forth.

MIRROR
The Evil Queen was so furious she immediately called for her Huntsman.

QUEEN
(Screaming.)
HUNTSMAN!!!!!!!!!

HUNTSMAN enters running. HE is a timid man dressed in grey and green. HE wears a green helmet.

HUNTSMAN
Yes my Queen?

QUEEN
Huntsman. Tomorrow I want you to lead Snow White deep into the Black Forest and kill her!

HUNTSMAN
But why my Queen? She is only a child!

QUEEN
You will do as I command Huntsman, or I will have you thrown into the deepest, darkest pit I can find, and you will stay there for the rest of your miserable existence! Do you understand me, Huntsman?

HUNTSMAN
Yes, my Queen. I understand.

> QUEEN exits. THE HUNTSMAN lingers, uneasy, then exits.

MIRROR
Early the next morning, as he had been instructed to do, the Huntsman took Snow White deep into the Black Forest, where he intended to kill her.

> LIGHTS: low and spooky. SNOW WHITE enters through the forest. SHE is wearing HER Princess costume. HUNTSMAN enters behind HER.

SNOW WHITE
Huntsman. Why have you brought me so deep into the Black Forest?

HUNTSMAN
Your stepmother...the Evil Queen, thought you might...well, she thought some fresh air might do you well Princess.

SNOW WHITE
Fresh air?

HUNTSMAN
Yes, smell that fresh air!
>(Inhales deeply, then coughs.)

SNOW WHITE
But it's so dark here in the forest...I can hardly see my hand in front of my face.
>(SHE turns away from the HUNTSMAN.)

MIRROR
The Huntsman knew that if he was going to do it, it would have to be now. He drew his sword.

>THE HUNTSMAN draws HIS sword.
>SNOW WHITE doesn't notice, though the audience will. SHE kneels down and HE raises HIS sword to strike.
>SHE turns and sees HIM, and is terrified.
>BOTH freeze.

MIRROR
But he couldn't do it.

>HUNTSMAN drops HIS sword and falls to HIS knees.

HUNTSMAN
I can't do it. Please forgive me Princess. The Queen...your stepmother is horribly jealous of you. She...ordered me to bring you deep into this forest and...kill you...but I couldn't do it. I could never harm you. I knew your father...he was a very good man... and my friend. But listen to me, you are not safe. You must run even deeper into the forest! Run until you can run no more, and you must never return! Do you understand me Princess?

SNOW WHITE
Yes, I think so.

HUNTSMAN
Run then. I'll tell the Queen the job has been done.

> SHE starts off, and then turns to HIM.

SNOW WHITE
Thank you, Huntsman. You really are a good man.

> SHE exits running.

HUNTSMAN
If the Queen learns of what I have done, I will really be a <u>dead</u> man.

> LIGHTS out on HUNTSMAN.

MIRROR
Snow White was so frightened by what the Huntsman had said that she ran over the hills and across the green until she could run no more. Exhausted, she fell fast asleep in the middle of the forest.

> LIGHTS dim, then rise on SNOW WHITE surrounded by FUZZY FOREST CREATURES. SHE stirs.

SNOW WHITE
Oh...good morning.

> THEY just look at HER. Pause.

SKUNK
You snore.

SNOW WHITE
I beg your pardon?

                    RABBIT
You snore.

                    DEER
Real loud.

                    CAT
Like a chainsaw.

                    SNOW WHITE
I do not.

                    DEER
You do too! Doesn't she everybody?

                    FUZZY FOREST CREATURES
Uh huh! Yep. Sure does. Like a chainsaw. Etc.

                    SNOW WHITE
Where am I?

                    WARTHOG
This is our home.

                    SNOW WHITE
And who are you?

                    CAT
We're The Fuzzy Forest Creatures. Maybe you've heard of us?

                    SNOW WHITE
No...at least I don't think so. Should I have?

                    CAT
Yeah, baby! We're the hottest act in the forest!

                    SNOW WHITE
Really?

                    CAT
Yep.

                    SNOW WHITE
Cool. Say, do you know somewhere I can hide? There's an
Evil Queen after me and I need to lay low for a while.

                    FUZZY FOREST CREATURES look at
                    EACH OTHER.

                    CAT
Yeah. We know a place.

                    SNOW WHITE
Can you take me there?

                    CAT
We thought you'd never ask!

                    THEY all put sunglasses on. MUSIC:
                    Something "funky". THEY exit, as LIGHTS
                    fade, then rise on Dwarf House. SNOW
                    WHITE enters with THEM.

                    SNOW WHITE
What a charming little house. I wonder if anyone's at home.

                    SHE walks through door.

                    SNOW WHITE
Hello? Is anyone there? My goodness, this place is an awful
mess. And everything is so short. I wonder if this house
belongs to children.
          (A thought occurs to HER.)
Maybe if I tidy up this house a bit, the children who live here
will let me stay for a while.

                    DANCE MUSIC. THEY clean/dance.
                    SNOW WHITE gets broom, dancing and

> singing. SHE sweeps, then exits. SHE re-enters with feather duster. SHE dusts, then exits. SHE re- enters with floor buffer, or if that isn't available, the plunger again. MUSIC ends. FUZZY FOREST CREATURES exit.

SNOW WHITE
Goodbye, little friends. Thank you.
> (Yawning.)

Gosh. All this house cleaning has made me very tired.
> (Pokes HER head in other room.)

Ahhh, how cute. Seven little beds. Maybe whoever lives here won't mind if I take a little nap.

> SHE exits with floor buffer. DWARF entrance music plays. THE SEVEN DWARVES enter, all wearing brown hooded robes, doing little dance step together and singing. THEY stop outside the cottage, and EACH ONE does something to indicate what THEIR name is. THEY enter cottage. THEY are muttering and grumbling, and then ALL stop at the exact same time and look around.

DWARF #1
Great oogly moogly!

DWARF #2
Someone's been here!

DWARF #3
Someone's cleaned the place up!

DWARF #4
Who would dare?

DWARF #5
Look at them dishes! They're clean!

DWARF #6
Someone did the dishes too?

DWARF #6 exits to other room.

DWARF #7
Unbelievable!

DWARF #1
My fellow Dwarves…I believe what we have here is one of them ghosts!

DWARF #2
A ghost that does dishes?

DWARF #3
I didn't know ghosts did dishes!

DWARF#4
How can you be so sure?

DWARF #1
Well, I know it wasn't the fuzzy forest creatures running around out there!

DWARF #5
Well, of course not. That would be silly.

DWARF #6
(From other room.)
Oh my gosh!

DWARF #7
What is it?

DWARF #6
Someone cleaned the toilet!

> ALL DWARVES rush into other room. A toilet is heard flushing.

DWARVES
(Offstage.)
Ooooooooooooooooo!

DWARF #7
(Offstage.)
Who would stoop so low?

DWARF #1
(Offstage.)
Maybe it was that girl sleeping in our bed over there.

> There is a beat.

DWARVES

GIRL!!!

> DWARVES come running back on in a panic screaming and running into EACH OTHER. SNOW WHITE enters.

SNOW WHITE
Wait a minute! What's wrong?

> DWARVES stop. Beat.

DWARF #2
It's a girl! Run!!!

> DWARVES run around again.

SNOW WHITE
Wait a minute! Wait a minute! Why are you so afraid of a girl?

DWARF #3
Because girl's have cooties!

> DWARVES run around again screaming "Cooties!"

SNOW WHITE
Stop running around and screaming! I can assure you that girls do not have cooties! I do not have cooties!

> DWARVES have settled down. Slowly THEY approach HER.

DWARF #4
Are you sure you don't have cooties?

SNOW WHITE
Certainly not. My name is Snow White. What are your names?

DWARF #1
My name is _____.

> HE uses the name the audience has given HIM, and acts out whatever it implies. Each DWARF steps forward and does the same thing in turn.

SNOW WHITE
Those are very…creative names.

DWARF #1
Don't blame us, we didn't pick 'em.
(Points to audience.)

SNOW WHITE
And do you midgets live here all alone?

>DWARVES look at each other.

DWARF #2
Excuse me?

DWARF #3
I'm sorry. Did she just call us midgets?

DWARF #4
I think she did!

DWARF #5
The nerve!

DWARF #6
We are not midgets!

DWARF #7
We're dwarves! Don't you know the difference?

SNOW WHITE
Why no…what is the difference?

DWARF #7
Uh…well, we dwarves…we're better dancers!

DWARVES
Yeah!

>CLASSICAL TYPE MUSIC plays and
>THEY dance.

SNOW WHITE
Gee. I never knew that about dwarves.

DWARF #1
I'm sure there's a lot you don't know about dwarves. And by the way, what are you doing in our house?

DWARVES
Yeah! Tell us! What's going on? What are you doing here? Etc!
>(NOTE: The same DWARF should say "Etc." each time.)

SNOW WHITE
>(Beginning to cry.)

Oh…it's so horrible!

DWARF #2
Ah…please don't cry Snow White…you'll make me cry.
>(HE does.)

>THEY all cry. Bawl actually.

DWARF #3
>(Crying.)

Why are we all crying?

DWARF #4
>(Crying.)

Because it's so darn sad!

SNOW WHITE
But you haven't even heard my story yet.

DWARF #5
>(Crying.)

Tell us! Tell us!

>THEY gather around HER. ALL blow THEIR noses simultaneously.

SNOW WHITE
Well, my Stepmother is the Evil Queen.

DWARF #6
Ooooh, she's evil!

SNOW WHITE
Yes, we've established that already. Anyway, she tried to have me killed, so I ran away.

DWARF #7
Where'd you run to?

THEY all look at HIM.

DWARF #1
Where do you think she ran away to nincompoop? She ran here.

DWARF #7
Oh yeah. That makes sense.

DWARF #1
Listen, Snow White, if you want to, you can stay with us. We won't let anything happen to you. Will we, fellas?

DWARVES
You bet! No problem! Sure! Glad to help! Etc.

DWARF #1
We were all great warriors once. In the days of the Old Republic.

DWARVES strike warrior poses.

DWARF #2
Wait a minute! She can't stay here.

                    DWARF #1
Why not?

                    DWARF #2
Because she's not a dwarf. And dwarf law states that only a dwarf can live in a dwarf house.

                    DWARF #1
She is kinda short.

                    SNOW WHITE
Hey!

                    DWARF #2
Not short enough. Plus she's way too skinny.

                    DWARF #1
Are you sure?

                    DWARF #2
As sure as I'm a dwarf.

                    DWARF #1
We'll just have to take you before the Council.

                    SNOW WHITE
The Council?

                    DWARF #1
The Council of the 47 Dwarves!

                    SNOW WHITE
Oh my!

                              LIGHTS dim, then rise very dramatically on
                              SNOW WHITE in a beam of light. 47
                              DWARVES surround HER.

JUDGE #1

State your name.

SNOW WHITE

Snow White.

DWARVES all whisper amongst THEMSELVES.

JUDGE #2

You stand before us accused of the heinous crime of not being a dwarf. How do you plead?

SNOW WHITE

Uh...guilty?

JUDGES all whisper.

JUDGE #3

And yet you wish to live among us? To be part of our community?

SNOW WHITE

I do.

JUDGE #4

Why?

SNOW WHITE

Because I feel safe here.

JUDGES whisper.

JUDGE #1

Young lady, in seven hundred and eleventy years, there has never been anyone live among us dwarves except us dwarves. And frankly, that's the way...

DWARVES

Uh huh! Uh huh!

JUDGE #1

…we like it.

DWARVES

Uh huh! Uh huh!

JUDGE #1

Besides, it's the law, and we take the law very serious here.

SNOW WHITE

So, I can't stay?

JUDGE #1

No, I'm afraid not dear. You simply aren't a dwarf.

DWARF #1

Wait a minute, Your Honor!

JUDGE #1

Yes, what is it?

DWARF #1

We dwarves have always been known for our generous spirits…our fierce loyalty…

DWARF #7

And don't forget we're great dancers too!

DWARVES

Yeah!

ALL dance, badly.

JUDGE #1

All of this is true, but what's your point? The law is the law.

DWARF #1

I understand. The law is the law. And the law states that only a dwarf may live among the dwarves...BUT...nowhere does it say that you have to be born a dwarf!

DWARVES all whisper.

JUDGE #1

Pardon me for saying this, but...huh?

DWARF #1

What if we..."naturalized" her?

SNOW WHITE

SAY WHAT???

DWARF #1

Trained her.

JUDGE #1

Trained her?

SNOW WHITE

Trained me for what?

JUDGE #1

Now see here. It's not that easy. Being a dwarf is a way of life. A spirit.

DWARF #1

We can make her better than she was. Shorter. Plumper. Fuzzier. And the cost will be only six million dollars.

DWARVES

SAY WHAT???

DWARF #1

Ok, ok. It'll only cost us a flannel shirt and a fake beard.

> DWARVES are satisfied. DWARF #2 and #3 put flannel shirt and beard on SNOW WHITE.

DWARF #1
Wow. You actually do look like a dwarf!

SNOW WHITE
Thanks. I think.

JUDGE #1
She does look the part. But she is going to need a dwarf name.

> EVERYONE looks at the audience.

DWARF #1
How about it? Can you help me pick out a dwarf name for Snow White?

> A name is selected that SNOW WHITE from the audience.

JUDGE #1
Now you are an official Dwarf _____. Good luck and may the dwarf be with you!

DWARF #1
Congratulations _____!

SNOW WHITE
Oh, thank you so very much!

> SHE kisses DWARF #1 on the head. The other DWARVES are dumbfounded.

DWARF #2
I hope she doesn't have cooties.

SNOW WHITE
I don't have cooties.

DWARF #1
(Lovey dovey.)
She doesn't have cooties.

DWARF #3
What?

DWARF #1
Nothing.

SNOW WHITE
If you are willing to let me stay here then I insist you let me earn my keep. I'll keep the cottage clean and I'll cook for you.

DWARVES
Cook?

DWARF #2
You mean real food? Like fried chicken?

DWARF #3
And cornbread?

DWARF #4
And taters? I love me some taters!

DWARVES
Mmmm, taters!

SNOW WHITE
And jam cake? Do you like jam cake?

DWARF #5
Ma'am...we adore jam cake.

SNOW WHITE
Then it's settled. Tonight for supper, we will have jam cake!

> The DWARVES do a little happy jam cake dance.

SNOW WHITE
Now while I whip up the jam cake it'll give you guys just enough time to wash up.

DWARVES
(To audience.)
WASH UP???

> BLACKOUT. LIGHTS: RISE on MIRROR. QUEEN stands before HIM.

QUEEN
Ok. Let's try this again. Magic Mirror on the wall, who's the fairest one of all?

MIRROR
Uh oh!

QUEEN
Are we going to do this again?

MIRROR
Well, you see…

QUEEN
Just tell me already!

MIRROR
Very well.
(Clears throat.)
"Over the river and across the green, Snow White's still fairer than you, my Queen."

QUEEN
SAY WHAT???

MIRROR
You asked.

QUEEN
How can this be?
(Yelling.)
HUNTSMAN!!!!!

HUNTSMAN enters.

HUNTSMAN
Yes, my Queen?

QUEEN
Huntsman. Do you remember that little job I asked you to take care of for me?

HUNTSMAN
(Being coy.)
Which job would that be, my Queen?

QUEEN
You know, the one where I asked you to take Snow White deep into the Black Forest and kill her.

HUNTSMAN
Oh…that job.

QUEEN
Yes. That job! Did you do it or not?

HUNTSMAN
(Thinking.)
Yes.

QUEEN
Yes…which?

HUNTSMAN
Not.

QUEEN
Not…what?

HUNTSMAN
You asked if I did it or not. The answer is not.

QUEEN
And why…not…may I ask?

HUNTSMAN
Well…

QUEEN
Never mind. I'm sure the answer would bore me anyway. Do you know the punishment for disobedience…or not?

HUNTSMAN
(Very scared.)
Not?

> SHE raises HER hands as if to cast a spell. LIGHTS: BLACKOUT. THE HUNTSMAN screams. LIGHTS: RISE on DWARVES standing around a wash tub looking into it.

DWARF #1
It's so…clean…and bubbly.

DWARF #2
Who's gonna go first?

DWARF #3
Not me. I had my bath already!

DWARF #4
When was that?

DWARF #3
Last April.

DWARF #5
Somebody has to get in.

DWARF #6
Who's it gonna be?

DWARF #7
Not me!

DWARVES
Not me! Not me! Not me! Etc.

DWARF #1
I know. Let's all get in at the same time.

THEY all look at HIM.

DWARVES
SAY WHAT???

DWARF #1
It's the only fair thing to do.

ALL shrug, then step in. If the tub is big enough, ALL sit down.

DWARF #1
Now see. This isn't so bad.

DWARF #2
Shouldn't we have taken our clothes off first?

                    DWARVES
Aaaaaaaaahhhh.

                    DWARF #3
Is this one of them whirlpool tubs I've heard so much about?

                    DWARF #4
I don't think so. Why do you ask?

                    DWARF #3
I was just wondering where all those bubbles were coming from.

> Beat. Then all DWARVES realize someone has farted.

                    DWARVES
EEEEEEEEEWWWWWWWWWW!!!

> THEY jump out of tub and run away. DWARF #6 stays in tub, looks at audience and grins. BLACKOUT. LIGHTS: RISE on QUEEN and VILLAINS.

                    QUEEN
Now listen, if you want something done right you have to do it yourself.

> In this scene, MIRROR keeps sticking HIS tongue out at QUEEN, but stops when SHE turns to look at HIM. VILLAINS find this amusing. SHE holds up a magic potion.

                    QUEEN
When I drink this magic potion it will transform me into a hideous old hag and Snow White will never be able to recognize me.

> SHE drinks potion. LIGHTS: go berserk.

> There is smoke. QUEEN puts on hag mask
> and hooded robe. SHE holds a sack.

CRUELLA

Impressive.

QUEEN

And now...
> (SHE reaches in sack and pulls out an apple core.)

Ok...who ate my apples?

> MIRROR and VILLAINS have been
> chewing something but now stop. SHE
> reaches into sack again.

QUEEN

Let's see what else we have in here.
> (Pulls out a kumquat.)

What's this?

MIRROR

That O' Queen, is a kumquat.

QUEEN

A kumquat? What's a kumquat?

WOLF

A kumquat is a subtropical, pulpy, citrus fruit, used chiefly for preserves.

QUEEN

How'd you know that?

WOLF

I saw it on Jeopardy.

QUEEN

Really? Well, it'll just have to do.

> SHE pours potion over it and waves HER hands, casting a spell. VILLAINS join in.

QUEEN
One bite of this poison...kumquat, and Snow White will sleep forever! Bwah-ha-ha-ha-ha!

VILLAINS
Bwah-ha-ha-ha-ha!

> BLACKOUT. LIGHTS: RISE on DWARVES and SNOW WHITE dancing and cleaning to music. MUSIC ends. THE DWARVES head off to work, EACH getting a kiss from SNOW WHITE and then exiting. DWARF #1 is last.

DWARF #1
Beware of strangers, Snow White. There's no telling what the Evil Queen will do if she finds out that you're still alive.

SNOW WHITE
Don't worry. I'll be careful.

DWARF #1
May the dwarf be with you!

> DWARF #1 starts off, then comes back for a kiss. SNOW WHITE begins to work. There is a knock at the door.

SNOW WHITE
I wonder who that could be.

> SHE opens door. QUEEN is standing there, in disguise.

QUEEN
Are you here all alone, girl?

SNOW WHITE
Why, yes. Who are you?

QUEEN
Just a little old lady happening by. Where are the other people who live here?

SNOW WHITE
They've gone to work for the day.

QUEEN
Excellent. Excellent.

> THE QUEEN walks right past SNOW WHITE into the cottage.

SNOW WHITE
I beg your pardon?

QUEEN
Never mind. And what are you doing this fine morning…oh, I didn't catch your name?

SNOW WHITE
Oh, it's…_____, and I was just about to bake a pie.

QUEEN
A pie?
    (To audience.)
How fortuitous!

SNOW WHITE
    (To audience.)
Fortuitous?
    (To QUEEN.)
How so?

QUEEN
Well, you see. I just happen to be carrying a basket full of yummy kumquats and I was wondering if you would like to have some for your pie?

SNOW WHITE
Kumquats? What are kumquats?

QUEEN
Well, they're a subtropical, pulpy, citrus fruit, used chiefly for preserves, but they also make great pies my dear.

SNOW WHITE
You know, I don't think I have ever had a kumquat pie before.

QUEEN
And what's more, these are very special kumquats.

SNOW WHITE
Really?

QUEEN
Absolutely! You see, these are magic, wishing kumquats!

SNOW WHITE
Really? Magic, wishing kumquats?

QUEEN
Of course. Would I lie?

SNOW WHITE
I have no idea. I just met you.

QUEEN
Oh, I'm very honest. Take my word for it. Would you be interested in making a special wish?

SNOW WHITE
Yes. Yes, I would.

QUEEN
Here you go.

> Hands SNOW WHITE a kumquat.

SNOW WHITE
It's a funny looking little thing, isn't it?

QUEEN
Don't judge it by its outside appearance, girl. You never know what it might be like on the inside…don't forget to make a wish.

> SNOW WHITE closes HER eyes and makes a wish.

QUEEN
Now take a bite.

SNOW WHITE
Ok.

> SHE bites into it. There is a pause as SHE chews . Then SHE chews some more. Then SHE chews some more. QUEEN looks at HER watch and whispers to HERSELF.

QUEEN
Come on…I don't have all day.

SNOW WHITE
You know…this tastes kind of like…urk!

> SHE falls to the floor.

QUEEN
Now my pretty little Princess, you will sleep forever! Bwah-ha-ha-ha-ha!

VILLAINS
Bwah-ha-ha-ha-ha!

BLACKOUT. LIGHTS: RISE on MIRROR.

MIRROR
Snow White had fallen into a deep, deep sleep. A sleep so deep that only the kiss of her one true love could awaken her.

PRINCE MUSIC plays. PRINCE enters.

PRINCE
That's my cue baby.

MIRROR
Hello Prince.

PRINCE
What's shakin' baby?

MIRROR
Oh, not much, thank goodness. I wouldn't want to get knocked off the wall.
(MIRROR laughs waaaaaay too long at HIS own joke.)

PRINCE
Yes. Ha ha. That's a good one.

MIRROR
Thanks. So what brings you here?

PRINCE
I'm looking for that cute chick that used to work here....uh, Snow White was her name, I think.

MIRROR
Well, Prince. She's over the river and across the green, but she's just been whammied by the Evil Queen.

PRINCE
Bummer.

MIRROR
Luckily, a kiss from her one true love can awaken her from her eternal slumber!

PRINCE
Really? Oh baby! Bring on the smooches!

> PRINCE takes a shot from HIS breath spray, then practices smooching technique.

HUNTSMAN
(Entering.)
Unfortunately, he isn't her one true love.

MIRROR
Huntsman! How did you escape the Queen's pit?

HUNTSMAN
It's a long story and we haven't much time.

MIRROR
What were you saying? Prince isn't Snow White's one true love?

HUNTSMAN
Absolutely not!

PRINCE
How can you possibly know that?

> HUNTSMAN whispers in PRINCE'S ear.
> MIRROR struggles to overhear.

PRINCE
Oh...gross!!!!!

> PRINCE spits and wipes tongue on arm.

MIRROR
Huntsman? Are you certain of this?

HUNTSMAN
I'm certain. I've known this family for many years. We must find Snow White immediately.

MIRROR
If what you've just told us is true, it may already be too late!

> BLACKOUT. LIGHTS: RISE on cottage. THE DWARVES stand around SNOW WHITE, who is laying on the table. There is a pause.

DWARF #1
Is she dead?

DWARF #2
No. She seems to be in a deep sleep.

DWARF #3
Can we wake her up?

DWARF #4
No. I've tried everything I can think of.
> (Tickles HER feet. No response.)

DWARF #5
> (Picking up half eaten kumquat.)

What's this?

DWARF #6
It's a half-eaten kumquat!

DWARF #7
Oh no! It's the old poison kumquat trick! I've seen it a million times!

DWARVES all agree.

DWARF #1
This is the work of the Evil Queen, I'll guarantee it!

HUNTSMAN
(Entering.)
You're right, but we might be able to save her still.

DWARF #1
Who are you?

HUNTSMAN
I'm the Huntsman, and this is Prince.

DWARF #2
Oh, we've heard of you.

HUNTSMAN
So, she's in a deep sleep?

DWARF #3
It seems that way.

HUNTSMAN
Then only one thing can awaken her. The kiss of her one true love.

DWARVES look at PRINCE.

PRINCE
Don't look at me. She's my sister.

DWARVES
SAY WHAT???

HUNTSMAN
It's true. Snow White had a brother who was raised by her uncle in the kingdoms to the north.

DWARF #4
All is lost then.

> There is a pause.

DWARF #1
Maybe not.

> DWARF #1 bends over HER and kisses HER gently. SHE stirs. Then puts HER arms around HIM and plants one on HIM. DWARVES cheer. Finally HE breaks free and SHE rises.

SNOW WHITE
What happened?

HUNTSMAN
The Evil Queen cast a spell over you Princess. Only the kiss of your one true love has awakened you.

> SNOW WHITE looks at PRINCE. HE shakes HIS head no. EVERYONE points to DWARF #1. HE blushes.

SNOW WHITE
Well, I always did like older men.

DWARF #5
We're not going to let the Evil Queen get away with this, are we?

SNOW WHITE
(Rising.)
Oh no. No more Miss Nice Princess. It's time for Snow White to Strike Back!

> BLACKOUT. LIGHTS: RISE on MIRROR and QUEEN.

QUEEN
Magic Mirror on the wall, who's the fairest of them all?

MIRROR
"You gave it your all you wicked Queen, but Snow White is coming to kick you're...
(Tries to think of a rhyme, but can't.)
...butt!"

QUEEN
Snow White? How is that even possible?

SNOW WHITE
(Who has entered.)
Oh, it's possible Stepmother!

> QUEEN turns to find SNOW WHITE holding blue bladed sword. SHE grabs a red bladed sword.

QUEEN
The Dwarves have taught you well, Snow White.

SNOW WHITE
They have.

QUEEN
Is it a final showdown that you're looking for, Princess?

SNOW WHITE
Darn tootin!

QUEEN

Then…so be it!

> ADVENTURE MUSIC. There is a massive battle between THE QUEEN and SNOW WHITE. DWARVES and VILLAINS enter and battle EACH OTHER. At one point, SNOW WHITE even pretends that HER hand has been cut off. Finally, SNOW WHITE gains both swords and chases THE QUEEN offstage. THE QUEEN screams loudly. BLACKOUT. BEAT.
> LIGHTS: RISE on THE MIRROR.

MIRROR

And so, with the Evil Queen vanquished, and peace restored to the kingdom, Prince went on to become a music superstar, winning numerous Grammies and finally changing his name to a weird unpronounceable symbol.

>   (PRINCE enters, blows audience a kiss.)

Snow White married her one true love, _____, and ironically, they had seven children of their own.

> (SNOW WHITE and DWARF #1 enter holding hands.)

No one in the Kingdom ever touched another kumquat as long as they lived, and finally, there was a large celebration in the castle in which everybody got down with their bad selves.

> CAST enters. FESTIVE MUSIC. The CAST dances.

THE END

CINDERELLA
AND THE
QUEST
FOR THE
CRYSTAL PUMP

BY
L. HENRY DOWELL

BLACK BOX THEATRE PUBLISHING

CAST

Touchstone
Prince Charming
The King
The Queen
Magic Mirror
Cinderella
Stepmother
Brumhilda
Grizelda
Cryer
Fairy Godperson
Dr. Thingamabob
Clockwork Cindy
Colonel Klamauk
Klink
Klank
Master Fuzzy
Fuzzy Forest Ninjas
Snow White
Little Dwarf #1
Little Dwarf #2
Sleeping Beauty
Pocahontas
The Little Mermaid
Rapunzel
Old Professor
Spiders

Cinderella and the Quest for the Crystal Pump

SCENE ONE

LIGHTS: RISE to reveal a beautiful palace. MUSIC:
Classical style fairy tale music plays.
TOUCHSTONE THE JESTER enters looking
around.

TOUCHSTONE
Yoo hoo! Prince Charming? Where are you? Your Majesty?
(Notices audience.)
Oh, hello there. Listen. Have you seen the Prince anywhere?
His parents are looking for him…again! My goodness, that
boy is always running off!
(Resumes looking.)
Prince Charming?

PRINCE enters, more zero than hero.

PRINCE
What is it, Touchstone?

TOUCHSTONE
There you are! Where have you been? The King and Queen
have been looking all over the place for you! Don't you
know what today is?

PRINCE
Yes, I am well aware of what today is.

TOUCHSTONE
(Looking off into the distance.)
Oh dear! Here come your parents!

MUSIC: Trumpet flourish as KING and
QUEEN enter.

KING
Prince Charming! We have been looking all over for you!

PRINCE
So I heard.

QUEEN
Don't you know what today is?

PRINCE
Yes mother. I know all too well what today is. My birthday

QUEEN
That's right. Your birthday!

> TOUCHSTONE blows a whirly gig. ALL shoot HIM a look.

TOUCHSTONE
Sorry.

KING
Where have you been, my son? Out slaying a dragon maybe?

QUEEN
Or rescuing a damsel in distress perhaps?

TOUCHSTONE
Or maybe fighting off an evil horde!

PRINCE
I was reading.

KING
Reading?

QUEEN
Reading?

####TOUCHSTONE

Reading?

####PRINCE

That's right. I was reading. I just wanted to find a nice quiet little corner of the castle where no one would bother me and enjoy a good book. Surely, that isn't a bad thing?

####KING

Certainly not. Reading is a fine thing. Many people read. In fact, I do it on occasion myself.

####TOUCHSTONE

You do?

####KING

(Shoots TOUCHSTONE another look.)

Of course I do.

####QUEEN

As do I. We were just hoping that maybe you were out doing something....I don't know....something...

####TOUCHSTONE

Less wimpy?

####KING

(Another look.)

More "princely". You are to be the ruler of this kingdom some day, and the people must be able to look up to you, my son. Your grandfather was a great dragon slayer. Everybody looked up to him. The tales of his greatness were made into songs. And my father, well, there was no finer horseman in all the land.

####QUEEN

And your father, Prince Charming...he risked life and limb to rescue me from an evil witch, deep within the Black Forest.

KING
Please dear!

QUEEN
You are too modest, my darling.

KING
No. I meant please, go on.

QUEEN
He was just a young prince then. Dashing and brave. And he won my heart that day.

The KING and QUEEN nuzzle.

PRINCE AND TOUCHSTONE
Eeeeewwwww, old people love!

KING
But today is your day my son. It's your…

PRINCE
Birthday. Yes, we've established that already.

QUEEN
Your father and I wanted to give you your gift as soon as you awoke, but we couldn't find you.

PRINCE
Here I am now.

KING
Indeed you are. Touchstone!

TOUCHSTONE
(Coming to attention and saluting.)
Yes, your Majesty?

KING
Go get the gift!

TOUCHSTONE
Yes, Sir! As you command! Right away, Sir!
> (But HE doesn't move. The KING shoots HIM another look.)

Oh...right!

> HE exits running.

KING
I think you are going to be most surprised with this gift. It's something very special.

PRINCE
Is it that new set of encyclopedias I asked for?

KING
No...wait, how are encyclopedias something very special?

PRINCE
They're special to me.

> TOUCHSTONE enters pushing large wrapped object.

TOUCHSTONE
Before he opens his gift, shouldn't we sing a certain song?

QUEEN
An excellent idea Touchstone.

TOUCHSTONE
> (To audience.)

Will you help us sing for Prince Charles Edward Tiberius Charming III? You will? Fantastic!

EVERYONE

Happy Birthday to you! Happy Birthday to you! Happy Birthday Prince Charles Edward Tiberius Charming III! Happy Birthday to you!

QUEEN

Now open your gift!

> PRINCE starts to tear open wrapping paper to reveal the head of the MAGIC MIRROR.

MIRROR

Here's Johnny!

PRINCE

Wow. It's furniture. That talks. And does Jack Nicholson impressions!

KING

It's a mirror!

QUEEN

It's a magic mirror!

PRINCE
(Sarcastically.)
Just what I've always wanted.

QUEEN

We found it at a garage sale!

PRINCE

Went all out, huh?

KING

Evidently, it has quite a bit of history attached to it. It once belonged to an evil queen.

PRINCE
This just keeps getting better.

QUEEN
The queen would use its magic for all sorts of purposes, dark and sinister.

KING
You'll find this mirror to be quite articulate.

QUEEN
And very well read.

MIRROR
That's me!

QUEEN
And extremely intelligent. Watch this. Magic Mirror on the wall, who's the fairest one of all?

MIRROR
(To the audience.)
I ain't no dummy!
(To the QUEEN.)
You O'Queen are the fairest in the land!

QUEEN
Oooooo, I just love this thing!

PRINCE
You keep it then.

QUEEN
No. It's your gift. Besides, I have your father to tell me how beautiful I am.

KING
It's true. You are a very lovely woman.

THEY nuzzle again.

PRINCE AND TOUCHSTONE
Eeeeewwwww, old people love!

QUEEN
It says other things too! Watch this. Magic Mirror on the wall, should we throw the Prince a masquerade ball?

MIRROR
As I see it, yes.

KING
Will there be cake at this masquerade ball?

MIRROR
Most likely.

QUEEN
Is that all you care about? Cake?

MIRROR
It is decidedly so.

THEY look at the MIRROR who just smiles.

PRINCE
Mother. Father. I thank you for your gift. It is a most unusual treasure, but the last thing I want is for someone to throw me ball!

TOUCHSTONE throws a beach ball at PRINCE. THEY shoot HIM another look.

TOUCHSTONE
What? It's a sight gag. I'm a jester. It's my job.
(THEY stare harder. HE pulls out a banana.)
Wanna see me slip on a banana peel?

ALL

NO!!!

KING

Prince Charming. If you stay cooped up here in the castle all the time, how in the world will you ever have any adventures?

PRINCE

Adventures are overrated.

QUEEN

How will you ever meet any girls?

PRINCE

Girls are overrated, too.

> THEY look at EACH OTHER.

QUEEN
(Looking at KING.)
But...what about...grandchildren?

PRINCE

Good grief. Not this again.

KING

Son. You aren't getting any younger.

TOUCHSTONE

No doubt about that!
> (THEY look at HIM.)

Sorry.

PRINCE

I'm only 38!

KING
And you've never even fought a dragon! Why when I was a young man…

PRINCE
No offense Father, but I'm not you.

QUEEN
Charles Edward Tiberius Charming III!

PRINCE
Charlie.

QUEEN
Excuse me?

PRINCE
We've been over this, Mother. I prefer to be called Charlie.

QUEEN
That's ridiculous. That would make you Charlie Charming. Who ever heard of a Prince named Charlie Charming?

> TOUCHSTONE snickers. THEY shoot HIM another look. HE stops.

TOUCHSTONE
Sorry.

KING
Son. Let us do this. Let us have the ball. It would mean a lot to your mother. We'll invite every eligible maiden in the kingdom and just see what happens. Ok? You never know. The "right" girl just might show up!

QUEEN
Please...Charlie? For me? You never know. Pleeeeeeeeeease?

PRINCE
(Giving in.)
As you wish, Mother.

> SHE kisses HIM on the head. QUEEN and KING exit.

PRINCE
(Turns to MIRROR.)
Mirror…what do you think? Will I ever find the "right" girl?

MIRROR
Reply hazy. Try again later.

PRINCE

That figures.
(To audience.)
Aw gee whiz! What have I gotten myself into now? The "right" girl? What does that mean anyway? No "left" girls? What does the "right" girl look like anyway? Would I know her if I ran into her on the street?
(Pauses, thinking.)
No. I'm not ready for this. I'm afraid of girls. I know! I'll run away!

TOUCHSTONE
You can't! The King and Queen, they're throwing you a masquerade ball! You can't just run away!

PRINCE
Of course I can. Just tell my parents I went out to slay a dragon…a big red one with all kinds of claws and teeth…and…oh…I know, tell them I went out to rescue a damsel in distress…or fight an evil horde…I don't know…tell them I went out to fight an evil horde of damsels and rescue a dragon in distress. Either way, I'm sure they'll be ecstatic. They'll forget all about this masquerade ball business.

TOUCHSTONE
Prince Charming. Charlie. Old buddy. Old pal. You know I cannot lie to the King and Queen. Make fun of them, yes. Fart in their presence, yes. But lie to them…no. I can't.

PRINCE
(Thinking.)
Come with me then.

TOUCHSTONE
What? Out there? In the real world?

PRINCE
Why not?

TOUCHSTONE
But…I'm a jester? I've been a jester my whole life. What would I do out there?

PRINCE
Who knows? Go in to politics maybe.

TOUCHSTONE
If we go…and we don't like it…can we ever come back?

PRINCE
Not according to Thomas Wolfe.

TOUCHSTONE
Who's that?

PRINCE
Nevermind.

TOUCHSTONE
Ok. I'll do it. Just so I can watch over you.

MIRROR
Hey…guys?

PRINCE

Mirror?

MIRROR

Can I go, too?

PRINCE

You want to come with us?

MIRROR

Sure. It beats hanging around here all the time.
 (Laughs way too long and way too hard.)

PRINCE

Yes. That's a good one. I guess with your ability to tell fortunes you might come in handy. You tell us. Magic Mirror on the wall, would it be to our advantage to take you along?

MIRROR

Ask again later.

PRINCE

What?

MIRROR

Better not tell you now!

PRINCE

What?

MIRROR

Most likely?

 THEY give HER a look.

MIRROR

Yes.

PRINCE
Good. Now if we are going out into the real world, we are going to need some disguises.

TOUCHSTONE
I have just the thing right here.
(Pulls mustaches out of pocket.)

PRINCE
Fake mustaches?

TOUCHSTONE
Yep!

THEY put them on. MIRROR too.

PRINCE
I look like Gene Shalit.

TOUCHSTONE
Who?

PRINCE
Nevermind. And now, we're off to find a life completely devoid of adventure and absolutely no girls whatsoever!

ALL
No girls whatsoever!!!

LIGHTS: BLACKOUT.

SCENE TWO

LIGHTS: RISE on Cinderella's cottage. CINDERELLA enters wearing work clothes. SHE sweeps and seems happy.

STEPMOTHER
(Offstage.)
Cinderella? Are you finished with that sweeping yet?

CINDERELLA
Not yet, Stepmother!

BRUMHILDA
(Offstage.)
Cinderella? Did you get that laundry done? I can't find my purple bloomers!

CINDERELLA
Not yet, Brumhilda!

GRIZELDA
(Offstage.)
Cinderella! Don't forget to wash the dishes!

CINDERELLA
Will do, Grizelda!

STEPMOTHER
And feed the fish!

BRUMHILDA
And milk the cow!

GRIZELDA
And mow the grass!

STEPMOTHER
And beat the rugs!

BRUMHILDA
And take out the trash!

GRIZELDA
And churn the buttermilk!

ALL
CINDERELLA!!!

CINDERELLA
Yes! I heard you! I'll get everything done I promise.
(To audience.)
Gee whiz! My life is so bland and boring! I just can't stand it sometimes! "Cinderella, do the dishes!" "Cinderella, beat the rugs!" "Cinderella, fold the laundry!" "Cinderella, churn the buttermilk!" I hate buttermilk! Am I crazy for wanting to know what's out…there? Beyond these walls?

STEPMOTHER enters.

STEPMOTHER
Cinderella. Come here and sit beside me.
(THEY sit.)
I know you have a lot of work to do.

CINDERELLA
Yes ma'am! I certainly do.

STEPMOTHER
Things have been very difficult ever since your beloved father disappeared.

CINDERELLA
I know.

STEPMOTHER
I want to do something to help you get all of your chores done.

CINDERELLA

That would be wonderful! Thank you so much!

STEPMOTHER

I want to give you some...advice.

CINDERELLA

Advice?

STEPMOTHER

You must learn to manage your time better, my dear. Multi-task. Learn to do two things at once. Like beating the rugs and churning the buttermilk at the same time. You do have two hands you know. Do you understand me, Cinderella?

CINDERELLA

I think so.

STEPMOTHER

Good. I'm so glad we had this little talk. Now get back to work!

    (CINDERELLA resumes cleaning.
    STEPMOTHER addresses audience.)

Have you ever noticed the bias in these stories against stepmothers? I just want to go on the record here as being against this sort of negative stereotyping. Stepmothers have a very difficult job you know. Blending two separate families together into one cohesive unit is tough enough, and when you factor in the mysterious disappearance of my husband, Henry. He was a famous explorer you know. Well, that sort of thing is apt to make any woman...grouchy. You know what I mean? It's not that I dislike Cinderella...

CINDERELLA

Stepmother, would you...

STEPMOTHER
(Yelling.)
In a minute Cinderella! Can't you see I'm doing my monologue!

CINDERELLA
Sorry.

STEPMOTHER
Where was I? Oh yes. It's not that I really dislike Cinderella. She just...I don't know...annoys the living crap out of me with all her sweetness! All her "pleases" and "thank yous" and "yes Ma'ams". I bet she was an honor roll student too.

CINDERELLA
I was.
(STEPMOTHER shoots HER a look.)
Sorry.

STEPMOTHER
Anyway...my point is, that it's a very difficult job and people shouldn't be so quick to judge us stepmothers, at least not till you've walked a mile in my expensive and highly fashionable footwear.

> SOUND: Doorbell rings. BRUMHILDA enters.

BRUMHILDA
Someone's at the door.

> SOUND: Doorbell rings. GRIZELDA enters.

GRIZELDA
Anybody going to get the door?

> SOUND: Doorbell rings. THEY look at CINDERELLA.

CINDERELLA
I'll get the door.

> SHE exits, then re-enters with CRYER.

CRYER
By order of the Royal Family…a masquerade ball will be held Saturday next in celebration of the birthday of Prince Charles Edward Tiberius Charming III! All eligible maidens living in the kingdom are hereby invited to attend.

STEPMOTHER
A ball?

BRUMHILDA
A ball?

GRIZELDA
A ball?

CRYER
A masquerade ball, to be precise.

STEPMOTHER
Anything in that notice about an age limit?

CRYER
No…but there should have been.

> CRYER exits.

STEPMOTHER
Snit.
  (To GIRLS.)
Hot dog! We're going to the big dance, girls!

BRUMHILDA
Excuse me?

GRIZELDA
Did you just say "we"?

STEPMOTHER
That's right. "We". Maybe the Prince's taste in women runs to the ever so slightly more mature.

BRUMHILDA AND GRIZELDA
Bwah-ha-ha-ha-ha!

STEPMOTHER shoots THEM a look.
THEY shut up.

BRUMHILDA AND GRIZELDA
Sorry.

STEPMOTHER
Let's face it. When you've got it, you've got it.

BRUMHILDA
I'm going to look gorgeous! There's no way the Prince will be able to resist me!

GRIZELDA
Are you kidding? He'll take one look at me and forget your name!

BRUMHILDA
He's mine! You hear me?

GRIZELDA
Over my dead body!

BRUMHILDA
That can be arranged you know!

GRIZELDA
Mother! Brumhilda just threatened me!

STEPMOTHER
I don't care. Just don't get any blood on the floor. Cinderella is far too busy to clean it up.
(CINDERELLA nods in agreement.)
Oh girls! There's so much to do! We have to find dresses and get our hair done.

CINDERELLA
Stepmother?

STEPMOTHER
Yes, Cinderella? What is it?

CINDERELLA
May I go to the masquerade ball, too?

STEPMOTHER
Excuse me?

CINDERELLA
I never get to go anywhere. It would only be for one night.

BRUMHILDA
Poor Cinderella!

GRIZELDA
She seems to think she'd have a chance at nabbing the Prince for herself!

ALL
Bwah-ha-ha-ha-ha!

STEPMOTHER
Is that true Cinderella? Do you think the Prince might fancy a girl as plain and ordinary as yourself?

CINDERELLA
Oh no. Of course not. It's not that at all. I would just like to get out of here for a while.

STEPMOTHER
Well, I suppose you could go, provided you can find a suitable dress. I will not have you embarrassing us by showing up at the Royal Palace in rags!

CINDERELLA
Of course not.

STEPMOTHER
You'll have to get all of your chores done first.

CINDERELLA
Yes, Ma'am.

STEPMOTHER
Very well. Come girls! We must go shopping!

BRUMHILDA AND GRIZELDA
Shopping!

THEY exit. CINDERELLA turns to the audience.

CINDERELLA
I just want to get out of here. See the world beyond these four walls. I want to travel and meet people. All kinds of people. I want to have adventures! <u>I want to go to that ball!</u> Is that too much to wish for?

THE FAIRY GODPERSON appears in a puff of smoke and music.

FAIRY GODPERSON
Why, no my dear. Not too much at all.

CINDERELLA
Who are you...and how did you get in here?

FAIRY GODPERSON
I am your Fairy Godperson. I go where I wish.

CINDERELLA
Fairy God "person"?

FAIRY GODPERSON
It's the world we live in my dear. Even the fairy tales are getting all politically correct.

CINDERELLA
Why are you here?

FAIRY GODPERSON
I am here to grant your fondest wish.

CINDERELLA
Really?

FAIRY GODPERSON
Hey, would I lie?

CINDERELLA
I don't know. I just met you.

FAIRY GODPERSON
Oh, I'm very honest. Take my word for it.

CINDERELLA
And you are here to grant my fondest wish?

FAIRY GODPERSON
Indeed. I'm a Fairy Godperson, it's what I do.

CINDERELLA
That's fantastic!

FAIRY GODPERSON
I thought you'd like that...and just what is your fondest wish Cinderella?

CINDERELLA
I wish to go to the ball!

FAIRY GODPERSON
The Prince's masquerade ball?

CINDERELLA
That's the one.

FAIRY GODPERSON
I see. You'll need a dress.

CINDERELLA
Of course.

FAIRY GODPERSON
A fabulous dress.

CINDERELLA
Please!

FAIRY GODPERSON
And we have to do something about your hair!

CINDERELLA
I figured.

FAIRY GODPERSON
And shoes!

CINDERELLA
Shoes?

FAIRY GODPERSON
You'll need some new shoes!

CINDERELLA
I do love new shoes!

FAIRY GODPERSON
Who doesn't? And we are not talking about any old shoes!

CINDERELLA
Oh no?

FAIRY GODPERSON
Oh no! For this you'll need the perfect shoes to accentuate that cute little footsie of yours! A pair of shoes befitting a princess!

CINDERELLA
A princess?

FAIRY GODPERSON
Indeed! For this you will require nothing less than the perfect pair of Crystal Pumps!

CINDERELLA
Oh my!!!

FAIRY GODPERSON
You will have to earn these things, Cinderella!

CINDERELLA
But how?

FAIRY GODPERSON
You must go on a quest! But it won't be easy!

CINDERELLA
My father used to say that "nothing worth having ever is". Easy that is.

FAIRY GODPERSON
Your father sounds like a wise man.

CINDERELLA
He is. Was. He was a famous explorer. He disappeared mysteriously some years ago.

FAIRY GODPERSON
Do not trouble yourself with such things right now, Cinderella. Keep your mind on the task at hand. It will be a grand adventure indeed, Cinderella!

CINDERELLA
But what about my stepmother? Won't she miss me? She'll never agree to let me go to the ball once she learns I've run away on this "grand adventure".

FAIRY GODPERSON
Hmmmm. I hadn't thought of that. I have an idea though.

HE pulls out a cell phone.

CINDERELLA
What's that?

FAIRY GODPERSON
This is called a cell phone. They'll be very big one day. I'm sending, what's called, a text.

CINDERELLA
Text?

FAIRY GODPERSON
OMG. Its a message of sorts. I'm contacting an associate of mine who might be able to help in this matter.

SOUND: Doorbell.

FAIRY GODPERSON
That'll be him!

CINDERELLA
That was fast.

FAIRY GODPERSON
Cinderella, may I introduce Dr. Thaddeus Thingamabob!

> DR. THINGAMABOB enters. HE is an elf inventor.

CINDERELLA
How do you do, Dr. Thingamajig?

DR. THINGAMABOB
Thingamabob. And I do very well. How do you do?

CINDERELLA
Very well thank you.

FAIRY GODPERSON
Dr. Thingamabob is an award winning elf inventor.

CINDERELLA
Oh really?

DR. THINGAMABOB
Yes. Two silvers and a bronze.

> Silence.

FAIRY GODPERSON
(To CINDERELLA.)
That was his attempt at humor.

CINDERELLA
Oh...ha-ha-ha-ha....so, you say he's an elf?

FAIRY GODPERSON
Yes. You'll note his pointy ears.

CINDERELLA
And just how is Dr. Thingamahooey going to help me?

DR. THINGAMABOB
Thingamabob. And I am going to replace you.

CINDERELLA
Excuse me?

FAIRY GODPERSON
Only temporarily, my dear. You will need someone to take your place while you are away.

CINDERELLA
Who could possibly do that?

DR. THINGAMABOB
Allow me to introduce my latest invention…

> HE pulls out a remote control. Twists some knobs. CLOCKWORK CINDY enters. SHE is a robot version of CINDERELLA.

DR. THINGAMABOB
I call her the Cinderella 3000…or Clockwork Cindy for short!

CINDERELLA
Clockwork Cindy?

FAIRY GODPERSON
She'll be the perfect stand in for you. No one will suspect a thing.

CINDERELLA
Can she talk?

FAIRY GODPERSON
Can she talk? What a question! Can she talk! Ha....she can talk, can't she, Doctor?

DR. THINGAMABOB
Of course!

> HE flips some switches.

CLOCKWORK CINDY
Ho-Ho-Ho!

> THEY give DR. THINGAMABOB a look.

DR. THINGAMABOB
Sorry.

> HE makes an adjustment to CLOCKWORK CINDY, and then pushes a button.

CLOCKWORK CINDY
I love to clean.
    (Pause.)
I love to bake.
    (Pause.)
Oooo, is that a new broom?

CINDERELLA
I don't sound like that.

FAIRY GODPERSON
Sure you do. Don't worry about a thing, Cinderella. Dr. Thingamabob here is a pro. He used to work at the North Pole.

CINDERELLA
Really? What happened?

DR. THINGAMABOB
Uh…it was too cold. Brrrrrr.

CINDERELLA
Ok. I guess I'm on my way then. Wish me luck!

FAIRY GODPERSON
And don't forget, you have to be back home by midnight!

CINDERELLA
Why midnight?

FAIRY GODPERSON
This is Children's Theatre honey. If these little kids have to sit here for more than ninety minutes they'll pee in their seats, and we don't want that.

CINDERELLA
No. Nobody wants that!

FAIRY GODPERSON
Oh, and before I forget, here is a map to aid you on your quest.
    (HE hands HER a map.)

CINDERELLA
Thank you! Goodbye!

FAIRY GODPERSON
Goodbye and good luck, my dear!

    CINDERELLA exits, waving.

DR. THINGAMABOB
She's going to need it.

FAIRY GODPERSON
No doubt.

CLOCKWORK CINDY

Ho-Ho-Ho.

LIGHTS: BLACKOUT.

SCENE THREE

LIGHTS: RISE on a street scene. CINDERELLA enters on one side reading a map. PRINCE enters on the other side reading a map, followed by MIRROR, and TOUCHSTONE. PRINCE and CINDERELLA run into EACH OTHER.

PRINCE AND CINDERELLA
Sorry!

PRINCE
It was my fault. I'm such a klutz.

CINDERELLA
No. I should watch where I'm going.

PRINCE
Where were you going?

CINDERELLA
Pardon?

PRINCE
My friends and I are kind of lost.

CINDERELLA
Me too, I'm afraid. I'm sorry, I didn't catch your name?

PRINCE
It's…Charlie. My name is Charlie.
(To MIRROR.)
This is my friend…Mario.

MIRROR
Hiya!

PRINCE
(To TOUCHSTONE.)
And this is his brother…Luigi.

TOUCHSTONE
Lets a go!

CINDERELLA
Those are very interesting names.

TOUCHSTONE
Don't blame us. We didn't pick 'em.

>   TOUCHSTONE and MIRROR give
>   PRINCE a dirty look.

CINDERELLA
My name's Cinderella. I'm very pleased to meet all of you.

PRINCE
The pleasure is all ours. Listen, my friends and I, we're not from around here. Do you think that maybe we could tag along with you for a while?

CINDERELLA
I don't know. I'm kind of on a quest.

PRINCE
A quest? Really? For what?

CINDERELLA
Shoes…I guess you could say.

PRINCE

Shoes?
    (To HIMSELF.)
That sounds pretty boring!
    (To CINDERELLA.)
We'd love to come along with you on your quest for shoes, if it's ok with you, Cinderella.

CINDERELLA

I suppose it would be all right. I'm searching for the perfect pair of Crystal Pumps.

PRINCE

Sounds fancy.

CINDERELLA

I'm going to the Prince's masquerade ball. I want to look my best.

PRINCE

The Prince's masquerade ball? Oh…that sounds like great fun.

CINDERELLA

I hope so. Every maiden in the kingdom will be there.

PRINCE

Probably. I hear the Prince's mother and father really want him to get married.

TOUCHSTONE

And have grandchildren!
    (PRINCE shoots HIM a dirty look.)
Sorry.

CINDERELLA

I wonder what the Prince is really like. He's probably a total jerk.

TOUCHSTONE and MIRROR snicker.

PRINCE
I hear he's a pretty nice guy. Isn't that right…Mario? Luigi?

MIRROR
Whatever you say, boss.

TOUCHSTONE
Let's a go!

CINDERELLA
I have no idea what I'd even say to the Prince if I did meet him. "What's shaking, Prince?" "How 'bout them Mets?"

PRINCE
Maybe you could just start out with "Hi. My name is Cinderella. Pleased to meet you."

CINDERELLA
Yeah. That might work. I'll remember that if it ever happens, which right now is very doubtful.

TOUCHSTONE
Oh, I don't know. I'd say the odds are better than you think.

CINDERELLA
You think so?

MIRROR
You may rely on it.

PRINCE
So, where are these Crystal Pumps that you're looking for?

CINDERELLA
According to this map, it's over the river and across the green.

PRINCE
Kind of a funny place for a shoe store, but what are we waiting on?
(To MIRROR and TOUCHSTONE.)
Guys?

MIRROR AND TOUCHSTONE
Let's a go!

THEY join hands and skip off.
COLONEL KLAMAUK, KLINK, and KLANK enter.

COLONEL KLAMAUK
Klink! Klank! Hast du gehort was ich gehort haben? (Klink! Klank! Did you hear what I heard?)

KLINK and KLANK
Ja, Colonel Klamauk! (Yes, Colonel Klamauk!)

COLONEL KLAMAUK
Sie sind auf deinem Crystal Pumps suchen! (They are looking for the Crystal Pumps!)

KLINK
Was fur ein Zufall! (What a coincidence!)

KLANK
So sind wir! (So are we!)

COLONEL KLAMAUK
Naturlich dumkopfe! Lasst uns ihnen zu folgen! (Of course dummies! Let's follow them!)

KLINK and KLANK
Ja, Colonel Klamauk! (Yes, Colonel Klamauk!)

THEY exit. LIGHTS: BLACKOUT.

SCENE FOUR

LIGHTS: RISE on a forest scene. CINDERELLA, PRINCE, MIRROR, and TOUCHSTONE enter slowly, looking around.

TOUCHSTONE
Wh…where are we?

CINDERELLA
According to this map, we are in the Black Forest.

PRINCE
And just why are we in such a scary place when we are supposed to be shoe shopping?

TOUCHSTONE
I thought we were going to the mall.

MIRROR
Me too. I wanted a slushy.

CINDERELLA
Evidently there's something here that will show us the way to the Crystal Pumps.

PRINCE
These better be some awesome shoes!

CINDERELLA
Oh, they are! I know it. They just have to be!

TOUCHSTONE
Look! Someone's coming. Someone really short.

MASTER FUZZY enters.

CINDERELLA
Uh…hi? Could you help us?

MASTER FUZZY
To me talking, you are?

CINDERELLA
Yes. I think. Huh?

MASTER FUZZY
My counsel, seek you?

TOUCHSTONE
Wow! This guy's grammar sucks.

MASTER FUZZY
Heard that, I did!

TOUCHSTONE
Sorry, I am.

CINDERELLA
This map led me here. It was given to me by my Fairy Godperson. I'm looking for...

MASTER FUZZY
Know I, what you seek. The Cavern of the Crystal Pump.

PRINCE
Cavern? Who puts a shoe store in a cave?

CINDERELLA
(To PRINCE.)
Shhhh.
(To MASTER FUZZY.)
Yes. We seek the way and we were hoping that you could help us...

MASTER FUZZY
Master Fuzzy, my name is, and help you, I will.

ALL

YAY!!!

MASTER FUZZY

After test, you pass.

ALL

SAY WHAT???

MASTER FUZZY

Worthy, you must be. Prove it, you must.

TOUCHSTONE

We're quite worthy I assure you, this guy is…

PRINCE elbows HIM.

PRINCE

…wondering what we might have to do to prove our worth, Master Fuzzy?

MASTER FUZZY

Battle, you must.

MIRROR

Oh poop!

TOUCHSTONE

I'm a lover! Not a fighter!

PRINCE

You want us to battle?

MASTER FUZZY

Repeat myself, I will not.

CINDERELLA

You really want us to fight to prove ourselves to you?

MASTER FUZZY
Repeat myself, I will not.

TOUCHSTONE
But you just…

PRINCE elbows HIM again.

PRINCE
Ok then. If you want us to battle…we'll battle.

HE grabs TOUCHSTONE and puts HIM in a headlock. THEY all battle EACH OTHER.

MASTER FUZZY
Morons.
(THEY stop.)
Among yourselves, do not fight.

CINDERELLA
Then who do we battle?

MASTER FUZZY
Them.

FUZZY FOREST NINJAS enter quickly and take a battle stance.

ALL
Oh poop!

MASTER FUZZY
Ready! Fight!

MUSIC: BATTLE MUSIC. Large fight. Eventually only CINDERELLA remains. MASTER FUZZY claps.

MASTER FUZZY
Most impressive, Cinderella.

CINDERELLA
Thank you. Will you help us now?

MASTER FUZZY
I will.

CINDERELLA
How do we get to the Cavern of the Crystal Pump?

MASTER FUZZY
No idea, have I.

CINDERELLA
What? You have no idea?

MASTER FUZZY
Nope.

CINDERELLA
Then, what was all of this for?

MASTER FUZZY
Enjoy a good fight, do I.

CINDERELLA
Thanks for nothing. Let's go guys.

MASTER FUZZY
Wait! Know the way, I do not. Know the way to the one who knows the way, I do.

TOUCHSTONE
Say what?

MASTER FUZZY
Seek you the one who went before.

CINDERELLA
Who is that? I don't understand.

MASTER FUZZY
Now go. Master Fuzzy other entertainment seeks.

> THEY start to exit.

PRINCE
Where are we going, Cinderella?

CINDERELLA
I'm not sure…but evidently, we're going to find out.

> THEY exit. THE FUZZY FOREST
> CREATURES back off stage. COLONEL
> KLAMAUK, KLINK and KLANK enter.

COLONEL KLAMAUK
Sie haben diesen weg gekommen!   (They came this way!)

KLINK
Ich bin angstlich!   (I'm scared!)

KLANK
Ich auch!   (Me too!)

COLONEL KLAMAUK
Wer ist das klienste Kreatur?   (Who is this little creature?)

KLINK
Er ist sehr fuzzy!   (He is so fuzzy!)

KLANK
Und niedlich!   (And cute!)

MASTER FUZZY
Into this forest, you should not have come.

>   FUZZY FOREST CREATURES enter
>   quickly.

                    ALL
Oh poop!   (Oh poop!)

>   LIGHTS: BLACKOUT.

SCENE FIVE

LIGHTS: RISE on Snow White's cottage. Similar to
     Cinderella's. CINDERELLA, PRINCE, MIRROR,
     and TOUCHSTONE enter.

CINDERELLA
You guys wait outside. I'll see if anybody's home.

PRINCE
Ok Cinderella. If you say so, but be careful.

CINDERELLA
I will.

> SHE knocks.

SNOW WHITE
(From offstage.)
Come on in.

> CINDERELLA enters cottage.

CINDERELLA
Hello?

> SNOW WHITE enters. Pregnant with hair
> up in curlers.

SNOW WHITE
Well hello there!

CINDERELLA
Snow White? Wow! I never thought I'd run into you way out here in...well...

SNOW WHITE
The boondocks?

CINDERELLA
I wasn't going to say that…but…yes.

SNOW WHITE
It's ok. I like it out here in the middle of nowhere. Very peaceful.
    (SOUND: Baby screams offstage.)
Most of the time. So, what brings you so deep into the black forest?

CINDERELLA
I'm searching for the Cavern of the Crystal Pump.

SNOW WHITE
The Crystal Pump? That's ironic.

CINDERELLA
Ironic? How so?

SNOW WHITE
There was a gentleman who came through here looking for the Crystal Pump. It was some time ago however.

CINDERELLA
Very interesting.

SNOW WHITE
May I ask you a question?

CINDERELLA
Of course.

SNOW WHITE
Why do you seek the Crystal Pumps?

CINDERELLA
I want to go to the Prince's ball.

SNOW WHITE
Looking for a "happily ever after"?

CINDERELLA
Maybe.

SNOW WHITE
There's nothing wrong with that. It's what we all look for. But just remember this…love isn't always found in a big castle in the arms of a prince. Sometimes it's right in front of us. Look at me. I fell in love with a dwarf and I couldn't be happier.

LITTLE DWARF #1 and #2 enter.

LITTLE DWARF #1
Mommy! He hit me!

LITTLE DWARF #2
I did not! She's lying!

LITTLE DWARF #1
I am not! He hit me!

LITTLE DWARF #2
Did not!

LITTLE DWARF #1
Did too!

LITTLE DWARF #2
Did not!

SNOW WHITE
Both of you! Go to your rooms!

LITTLE DWARVES
Yes, Mommy.

THEY run offstage.

CINDERELLA
Happily ever after?

SNOW WHITE
Oh sure. No one ever tells you what that means when you're a little girl growing up. Diapers. The mortgage. PTA meetings. Don't get me wrong, Cinderella, I love my life. Six little dwarves...
    (Pats HER belly.)
...and one on the way. I wouldn't trade places with anybody.

LITTLE DWARVES
    (Offstage.)
Mommy!!!

SNOW WHITE
Don't make me come in there!

Silence.

Other PRINCESSES enter.

SNOW WHITE
Why hello girls! You remember Cinderella?

PRINCESSES
Hello. Yes of course. Good to see you. Etc.

CINDERELLA
Hello girls.

SNOW WHITE
Cinderella is on a quest!

POCAHONTAS
You go, girlfriend!

RAPUNZEL
What are you questing for?

CINDERELLA
The Crystal Pumps.

PRINCESSES
Gasp!

SLEEPING BEAUTY
Wow! When you quest, you don't fool around.

THE LITTLE MERMAID
Is there a man at stake?

POCAHONTAS
A prince maybe?

REPUNZEL
A "charming" prince?

CINDERELLA
Maybe. We'll see.

SLEEPING BEAUTY
(Yawning.)
Believe me Cinderella, we understand. Don't we, girls?

PRINCESSES
You better believe it. That's right. Ain't that the truth? Etc.

CINDERELLA
Mostly I just want to get out of the house. See the world a little bit.

SNOW WHITE
I remember those feelings. My stepmother used to keep me locked up in the palace cleaning all the time. I couldn't wait to get out and live a little bit.

LITTLE DWARVES
Mommy!!!

SNOW WHITE
I'm counting to three. ONE...
> (Silence.)

We're having a bridge game, if you want to stay and play a hand.

CINDERELLA
No, thank you! I've got a quest to get back to!

SNOW WHITE
Good luck, Cinderella. I hope you find what you're looking for.

PRINCESSES
Goodbye Cinderella! Take care! Good luck! Etc.

> CINDERELLA exits. PRINCESSES sit and play cards. LIGHTS: BLACKOUT.

SCENE SIX

LIGHTS: RISE dimly on cave. Lots of fog. CINDERELLA, PRINCE, TOUCHSTONE, and MIRROR enter.

MIRROR
We made it. The Cavern of the Crystal Pump!

TOUCHSTONE
How do you know this is the right cave?

MIRROR
There's a sign over there that says "Welcome to The Cavern of the Crystal Pump".

> THEY look and sure enough, there's the sign.

ALL
Oh yeah! Look at that! There is a sign! Etc!

TOUCHSTONE
This place is really spooky!

PRINCE
You can say that again.

TOUCHSTONE
This place is really spooky!

PRINCE
How did I know you were going to say that?

TOUCHSTONE
That's me. A reliable source of comic schtick! Would you like to see me slip on a banana peel?

ALL
NO!!!

CINDERELLA
What's that over there?

> SHE crosses to a wall and takes a parchment from it and blows off the dust.

PRINCE
What is it?

CINDERELLA
It looks like a riddle.
> (Reads.)

I run over fields and woods all day.
Under the bed at night, I sit alone.
My tongue hangs out, up and to the rear,
Waiting to be filled in the morning.
What am I?

> LIGHTS: RISE to reveal letters on the floor.

MIRROR
What's that all about?

> COLONEL KLAMAUK, KLINK and KLANK enter with swords.

COLONEL KLAMAUK
Ich werde Ihnen sagen, worum es geht!   (I'll tell you what it's about!)

> THEY look at EACH OTHER, confused.

PRINCE
I'm sorry. We don't speak whatever language that is you're speaking.

MIRROR
That's not exactly true.

PRINCE

Mirror?

MIRROR

Along with being very articulate and quite well read, I'm also fluent in over 30 languages.

TOUCHSTONE

You never told us that!

MIRROR

You never asked.

PRINCE

What is he saying then?

MIRROR

He said, "I'll tell you what it's about!"

COLONEL KLAMAUK

Sie müssen das Rätsel um Rechtschreibung aus der Antwort auf den Boden zu beantworten. Eine falsche Bewegung und du bist tot! (You must answer the riddle by spelling out the answer on the floor. One wrong move and you are a goner! Bwah-ha-ha-ha-ha!)

MIRROR

"You must answer the riddle by spelling out the answer on the floor. One wrong move and you are a goner! Bwah-ha-ha-ha-ha!"

PRINCE

What do they want?

MIRROR

Was wollen Sie? (What do you want?)

COLONEL KLAMAUK
Was denkst du wir wollen, Dummkopf? (What do you think we want, you fool?)

MIRROR
What do you think we want, you fool?

PRINCE
Mirror!

MIRROR
Sorry.

COLONEL KLAMAUK
Wir wollen die Crystal Pumps! (We want the Crystal Pumps!)

MIRROR
They want the Crystal Pumps!

PRINCE
That part we understood. But why?

MIRROR
Warum? (Why?)

COLONEL KLAMAUK
Es ist für unser furchtloser Anführer. Er will deinen Crystal Pumps für sich. (It's for our fearless leader. He wants the Crystal Pump for himself.)

KLINK
Yeah! Er mag in Frauenkleidern zu kleiden. (Yeah! He likes to dress in women's clothing.)

KLANK
Und singt Broadway Melodien! (And sing showtunes!)

MIRROR
They said it's for their fearless leader. He likes to dress in women's clothing and sing showtunes.

CINDERELLA
That's very weird.

COLONEL KLAMAUK
Lesen Sie die Rätsel wieder!   (Read the riddle again!)

MIRROR
He wants you to read the riddle again.

CINDERELLA
I run over fields and woods all day.
Under the bed at night, I sit alone.
My tongue hangs out, up and to the rear,
Waiting to be filled in the morning.
What am I?

Colonel Klamauk
Hmmmmmm.

TOUCHSTONE
What could it mean?

CINDERELLA
Shoes!

PRINCE
Shoes?

TOUCHSTONE
Shoes?

MIRROR
Shoes?

COLONEL KLAMAUK

Shoes?

KLINK

Shoes?

KLANK

Shoes?

COLONEL KLAMAUK

Of course...the letter "S"!

> HE steps on the letter "S". There is a
> rumbling. THREE GIANT SPIDERS enter
> and drag HIM off screaming.
> KLINK and KLANK run off screaming.

CINDERELLA

Only the riddle is written in ancient Hebrew, and everybody knows that in ancient Hebrew the word for shoe begins with an "N".

PRINCE

You can read ancient Hebrew?

CINDERELLA

Of course. Can't you? My father taught me.

PRINCE

Impressive.

OLD PROFESSOR
(From offstage.)
I agree. It is impressive. You have learned your lessons well!

> HE enters. Very old and grey. Wearing a
> fedora and a leather jacket.

CINDERELLA
Father?

OLD PROFESSOR
It's me, Cinderella.

CINDERELLA
When you didn't come back, we assumed you'd been killed.

OLD PROFESSOR
Dead? No. Just trapped in this cave by those giant spiders.

CINDERELLA
How did you survive all this time?

OLD PROFESSOR
Dried kumquats.

CINDERELLA
What's a kumquat?

OLD PROFESSOR
A kumquat is a subtropical, pulpy, citrus fruit, used chiefly for preserves.

CINDERELLA
I never knew that.

MIRROR
I did.

OLD PROFESSOR
I always pack my pockets full of them when I'm on a quest. Would you like some?

CINDERELLA
Uh…no. I ate before I left.

OLD PROFESSOR
Cinderella. I've got to know. Your stepmother…is she still the same sweet, lovable girl I left behind?

CINDERELLA
No, Father…she's been sort of…grumpy since you disappeared to tell you the truth.

OLD PROFESSOR
I can't wait to see her again. That is, if we ever get out of here.

CINDERELLA
We'll get out of here together, Father.

OLD PROFESSOR
How will we? We can't go back. Only forwards.

CINDERELLA
That's all right. I'm not leaving without the Crystal Pumps.

OLD PROFESSOR
Like father, like daughter. But if we're going to do this, Cinderella, then let's do it right.
(Pulls out a fedora.)
Welcome to the family business.

> HE places the fedora on HER head. MUSIC: Adventure music plays. There are a series of small scenes depicting the GROUP tiptoeing across the floor. Running from SPIDERS. Taking a dance break, running, ducking, and covering. Finally removing, slowly, the crystal pumps from a pedestal and replacing with a television. THEY look around. Nothing. THEY smile and congratulate EACH OTHER. Then there is smoke and SPIDERS. THEY run helter skelter in all directions. LIGHTS: BLACKOUT.

SCENE SEVEN

LIGHTS: Rise on Cinderella's cottage. STEPMOTHER, BRUMHILDA and GRIZELDA are tied up. CINDERELLA enters.

CINDERELLA
Stepmother? What happened?

SHE unties THEM.

STEPMOTHER
It was Cinderella…not you…the other Cinderella…she's evil. At first we thought she was you…

BRUMHILDA
But then she was all like "Do this!" and "Do that!"

STEPMOTHER
Feed the fish!

BRUMHILDA
Milk the cow!

GRIZELDA
Mow the grass!

STEPMOTHER
Beat the rugs!

BRUMHILDA
Take out the trash!

STEPMOTHER
Churn the buttermilk! Oh, how I hate buttermilk!

ALL
Buttermilk!!!

THEY start bawling.

CINDERELLA
Stepmother. I found someone. I think you might know him.

OLD PROFESSOR enters.

STEPMOTHER
Henry? Is that you?

OLD PROFESSOR
It's me…and stop calling me that.

STEPMOTHER
Where have you been all this time?

OLD PROFESSOR
Trapped in the Cavern of the Crystal Pump by a bunch of giant, man-eating spiders.

STEPMOTHER
How did you keep from going mad?

OLD PROFESSOR
I did what any man would do in that situation. I tried on women's shoes.

STEPMOTHER
You poor thing!

OLD PROFESSOR
I'll never understand how you women can walk in those blasted things!

STEPMOTHER
Oh, Henry!

OLD PROFESSOR
I told you to stop calling me Henry!

STEPMOTHER
But that's your name.

OLD PROFESSOR
I prefer to be called…"Indiana"!

STEPMOTHER
But honey, we named the dog Indiana!!!

ALL laugh.

CINDERELLA
Where did Clockwork Cindy go?

BRUMHILDA
She went to the ball!

GRIZELDA
She left with some pointy eared midget!

CINDERELLA
Dr. Thingamahoochie!

ALL
THINGAMABOB!!!

CINDERELLA
Whatever.

STEPMOTHER
They're up to no good Cinderella! They were talking about overthrowing the King and Queen and ruling the kingdom!

CINDERELLA
This is all my fault.

BRUMHILDA
So? Are we going to the ball or not?

GRIZELDA
Yeah? We're not going to let Clockwork Cindy get away with this, are we?

CINDERELLA
No. We're not! I've got the Crystal Pumps and nothing is going to keep me from going to the ball!

LIGHTS: BLACKOUT.

SCENE EIGHT

LIGHTS: RISE on palace. The KING and QUEEN are tied
    up. DR. THINGAMABOB and CLOCKWORK
    CINDY wear THEIR crowns. DR.
    THINGAMABOB'S is way too big and keeps
    falling down. ALL wear masquerade masks.

DR. THINGAMABOB
Well-well-well! Who ever knew taking over the kingdom would be so easy!

CLOCKWORK CINDY
Ho-Ho-Ho!

DR. THINGAMABOB
Remind me to adjust your vocal mechanism later.

CLOCKWORK CINDY
Ho-Ho-Ho!

DR. THINGAMABOB
That's right, baby! And there's nobody who can stop us! Bwah-ha-ha-ha-ha!

CINDERELLA enters.

CINDERELLA
Not so fast Dr. Thingamadoodle!

DR. THINGAMABOB
Thingamabob!

CINDERELLA
Whatever.

DR. THINGAMABOB
Cinderella?

CLOCKWORK CINDY

Ho-Ho-Ho?

CINDERELLA

Thought you could just waltz into the ball and take over the kingdom, huh?

DR. THINGAMABOB

Something like that.

CINDERELLA

Well, you thought wrong. Surrender!

DR. THINGAMABOB

Or what? You'll bake me a pie? Clockwork Cindy! Attack!

> THEY remove shoes and battle. Evenly matched. Just when it seems CINDERELLA is finished, the PRINCE enters, wearing a mask. HE fights CLOCKWORK CINDY.

DR. THINGAMABOB

Who is that?

> TOUCHSTONE and MIRROR have entered and are trying to free the KING and QUEEN.

TOUCHSTONE AND MIRROR

It's Prince Charming!

KING AND QUEEN

Prince Charming?

DR. THINGAMABOB

Prince Charming?

CINDERELLA

Prince Charming?

CLOCKWORK CINDY

Ho-Ho-Ho?

PRINCE

That's right!
>(Hands CINDERELLA HER sword.)

Here's your sword, Cinderella.

CINDERELLA

You know my name? How?

PRINCE

Everybody knows the daughter of the world's most famous explorer! Nice shoes by the way!

CINDERELLA

Thanks!

>THEY continue to fight until the BAD GUYS are vanquished.

QUEEN

Oh Charlie! We are so proud of you!

KING

Yes, Son! Very heroic! I think there might be a song in your future!

PRINCE

Thank you.

KING

And who is this young lady?

CINDERELLA

My name is…
>(Clock strikes twelve.)

Oh no! Midnight! My time is up!

SHE starts to run out.

PRINCE
Wait, Cinderella. I need to tell you something.

CINDERELLA
I can't stay. Please. It's not you. It's me.

ALL groan.

CINDERELLA
I think you are a very nice guy and a pretty good swordsman and all, but you see, I'm in love with someone else.

PRINCE
What?

CINDERELLA
I wanted to come here and meet you, but along the way I met another guy. I need to go find him and tell him how I feel.

PRINCE
I see. Do what you must, but don't forget these.

HE hands HER the CRYSTAL PUMPS.

CINDERELLA
Thank you.

PRINCE
And don't forget this.

HE places the fedora on HER head.

CINDERELLA
How did you…?
  (HE removes mask.)
Charlie? Why did….I didn't…I…Hi. My name is Cinderella. Pleased to meet you.

> THEY kiss.

CINDERELLA
Your name is Charlie?

PRINCE
Yep.

CINDERELLA
Charlie Charming?

PRINCE
Yep. Interested in becoming Mrs. Charlie Charming?

CINDERELLA
I think I might keep my maiden name.

PRINCE
What's that?

CINDERELLA
Jones.

> SHE winks at the audience. MIRROR comes forward.

MIRROR
And so, with peace restored to the kingdom...

FAIRY GODPERSON
(Offstage.)
Wait!

> HE enters with HIS usual flourish.

CINDERELLA
It's my Fairy Godperson!

FAIRY GODPERSON
You are not narrating this show, Magic Mirror.

MIRROR
Sorry.

FAIRY GODPERSON
In fact, I think your narrating days are behind you. Magic Mirror on the wall, what's your fondest wish of all?

MIRROR
Well...I'd like to be a real girl.

FAIRY GODPERSON
Very well. Bippity-boppity...oh, to heck with it! Come on out from behind the wall.

MIRROR comes out.

MIRROR
I'm a real girl! I'm a real girl!

TOUCHSTONE
Ok, Pinocchio...here...
(Hands HER a handkerchief.)
Wipe your face off. What about me Fairy Whatever? Do I get a wish?

FAIRY GODPERSON
Of course, dear Touchstone. What do you desire most?

TOUCHSTONE
Uh..........

MIRROR
Now he's speechless.

FAIRY GODPERSON
How about your very own HBO Comedy Special?

TOUCHSTONE

Uh……….

FAIRY GODPERSON
You're welcome. My good King and Queen?

> KING and QUEEN look at EACH OTHER.

KING and QUEEN
Grandchildren!

> EVERYONE looks at PRINCE and
> CINDERELLA.

FAIRY GODPERSON
Uh...I'll get back to you on that one.
    (Changes subject.)
What about you, Cinderella? What is your heart's fondest desire?

CINDERELLA
My wish already came true.

> SHE dips the PRINCE and kisses HIM.

FAIRY GODPERSON
And of course, they all lived happily ever after. Now, is this a party or what? Music please!

> MUSIC: Something festive. EVERYBODY
> gets down with THEIR bad selves.

THE END

RAPUNZEL

Escape from Zombie Tower

By

L. Henry Dowell

BLACK BOX THEATRE PUBLISHING

CAST

Rapunzel
King
Queen
Little Rapunzel
Little Rick Grimey
Little Negan
Brave Knight
Handsome Prince
Mother Negan
Abraham
Sneaky Glenn
Doctor Maggie
Marlene Dixon
Darlene Dixon
Granny Carol
Michelin
Rick Grimey
Judith Grimey
Coral Grimey
Lucille
Tiger
Zombies

Rapunzel: Escape from Zombie Tower

LIGHTS: Rise on a forest. RAPUNZEL enters and
    addresses the audience.

RAPUNZEL
The story you are about to hear is true. Every word of it.
    (LIGHTS: Rise on KING and QUEEN. KING
    carries baby tiger.)
Once upon a time, there was a wise, old King and his lovely
Queen.

QUEEN
Wise guy, is more like it.

KING
Did you call me wise guy? And did she call me old?

QUEEN
Yes, I did. And she did. And…she called me lovely.

KING
I'm not that old!

RAPUNZEL
You aren't supposed to see me.

QUEEN
Why not? You're standing right there.

RAPUNZEL
No, I'm not.

    KING and QUEEN look at EACH OTHER.

KING
What are you talking about, dear? We can clearly see you
standing over there, talking to those people.

QUEEN
Yes…who are those people? They look very odd. And why are they dressed so strangely? That's not proper attire to attend an audience with the King and Queen.

KING
Is there a dress code, my Queen?

QUEEN
Only for peasants, my King.

KING
Are they peasants?

QUEEN
Yes, every last one of them.

KING
Splendid! I consider myself the "People's King" but I so seldom get to rub elbows with "the people".

QUEEN
Well, there they are. Get to rubbing.

KING
Heck no. They look so…grubby.

RAPUNZEL
Can we get back to the story?

QUEEN
Oh, certainly!

KING
So sorry, dear!

RAPUNZEL
As I was saying, the royal couple was childless and this made them despair.

KING AND QUEEN

Sigh.

RAPUNZEL

This is where the story take a bizarre twist!

KING AND QUEEN
(With enthusiasm.)

Zombies!

RAPUNZEL

No. Lettuce.

KING AND QUEEN

Lettuce?

RAPUNZEL

Rapunzel Lettuce to be exact.

KING

Rapunzel Lettuce…what is that?

RAPUNZEL

It is an aromatic, often nutty-tasting green that has a high level of vitamin C, beta-carotene, vitamin B6, folic acid, iron, and potassium. But that isn't important right now. You see, the Queen loved salad!

QUEEN

It's good, and good for you!

RAPUNZEL

The King did not agree.

KING

Salad is the food that food eats.

QUEEN

Will you fetch me some foliage, dear?

KING
Yes, dear. What dressing would you prefer?

QUEEN
Kumquat dressing, please.

KING
On the side?

QUEEN
You know me so well.

THEY exit.

RAPUNZEL
Little did they know that the lettuce the Queen would ingest was picked from a magic garden, and so, nine months later…

SOUND: Baby crying.

RAPUNZEL
A little baby was born…me!

KING and QUEEN enter with baby with extremely long blonde hair.

KING
What a head of hair!

QUEEN
WORST. HEARTBURN. EVER!

RAPUNZEL
My parents, the King and Queen, soon discovered something else…my long hair was magic!

KING AND QUEEN
Magic?

                    RAPUNZEL
That's right. Anyone who was bound by my golden hair was compelled to tell the truth!

> The QUEEN looks at the KING. HE looks scared. SHE ties HIM up with the baby's hair.

                    QUEEN
Who ate the last piece of chocolate cake last night?

                    KING
I did.

                    QUEEN
Does this dress look nice on me?

                    KING
Not really.

                    QUEEN
Do you like my mother?

                    KING
Absolutely not. No. No. No.

                    RAPUNZEL
I didn't see much of my father after that. I grew up playing with other kids with special abilities whose mothers had also consumed the magic lettuce.
        (LITTLE RAPUNZEL enters.)
That's me.
        (LITTLE RICK GRIMEY enters.)
That's my friend, Little Rick Grimey. He had the ability to grow the most impressive beard, even in Kindergarten.

                    LITTLE RICK
How many times do I have to tell you, I'm in fourth grade!

LITTLE NEGAN enters.

RAPUNZEL
That was my other friend, Little Negan.

LITTLE NEGAN
Hello everybody! I'm Little Negan!

RAPUNZEL
Along with a flair for the melodramatic she had the power to bring the dead back to life as mindless zombies.

ZOMBIE enters, chases LITTLE RAPUNZEL and LITTLE RICK.

ZOMBIE
Brains! Brains! Brains!

LITTLE NEGAN
(To audience.)
Ain't I a little stinker?

THEY continue to chase EACH OTHER around and then exit.

RAPUNZEL
Those were good times. A little terrifying, but good times. We were inseparable, until one day…

LITTLE RAPUNZEL, LITTLE RICK and LITTLE NEGAN enter.

LITTLE NEGAN
Tell us, Little Rick!

LITTLE RICK
No!

LITTLE RAPUNZEL
Yes, tell us!

LITTLE RICK
NO! Leave me alone!

LITTLE RAPUNZEL AND LITTLE NEGAN
Which one of us do you like the best?

LITTLE RICK
I like you both the same!

LITTLE NEGAN
I want you to be my boyfriend!

LITTLE RAPUNZEL
I want you to be MY boyfriend!

LITTLE RICK
I'm only in fourth grade. I don't even like girls. You're all crazy as far as I'm concerned.

LITTLE NEGAN
I know, we'll tie you up with Little Rapunzel's magic hair and you'll have to tell the truth!

LITTLE RAPUNZEL
That doesn't seem very nice, Little Negan.

LITTLE NEGAN
Give me your hair, Little Rapunzel.

LITTLE RAPUNZEL
No. This isn't right and I won't let you use my magic hair this way.

LITTLE NEGAN
I thought you were my friend, Little Rapunzel! But if you want to be enemies...that's just fine with me!

> SHE raises HER arms in the air. ZOMBIES enter.

LITTLE RICK
On no! Zombies!

LITTLE RAPUNZEL
What should we do?

LITTLE RICK
Climb up in the tower, Little Rapunzel. I'll lead the zombies away.

> LITTLE RAPUNZEL climbs the tower.

LITTLE RAPUNZEL
Thank you, Little Rick!

LITTLE RICK
Hey, you stupid, brain-eating zombies! Bet you can't catch me!

> ZOMBIES seem offended, and chase HIM offstage. LITTLE RAPUNZEL climbs down.

LITTLE NEGAN
Where do you think you're going, Little Rapunzel?

LITTLE RAPUNZEL
Back to the palace to tell my parents what you tried to do!

LITTLE NEGAN
Oh no! We can't have that. Zombies!

>   SHE raises HER arms again. ZOMBIES
>   enter.

                    ZOMBIES
Brains! Brains! Brains!

                    LITTLE NEGAN
Back up you go, Princess! I can summon endless zombies to guard this tower! You'll be my prisoner forever and then I'm going to burn this kingdom to the ground! BWAH-HA-HA-HA-HA!!!

>   LITTLE NEGAN exits, LITTLE
>   RAPUNZEL sticks HER head out of the
>   tower.

                    LITTLE RAPUNZEL
This stinks.

                    RAPUNZEL
Tell me about it.
          (Pause.)
The King and Queen were heartbroken.

>   KING and QUEEN enter.

                    KING AND QUEEN
Sigh.

>   ZOMBIES chase THEM off.

                    RAPUNZEL
Over the years, many brave knights attempted to save me from the tower.

>   BRAVE KNIGHT enters.

                    BRAVE KNIGHT
Rapunzel! Rapunzel! Let down your long hair!

>LITTLE RAPUNZEL lets down HER hair but before the BRAVE KNIGHT can climb the tower, ZOMBIES attack and drag HIM off.

RAPUNZEL
Sometimes a handsome prince would try.

>HANDSOME PRINCE enters.

HANDSOME PRINCE
Rapunzel! Rapunzel! Let down your long hair!

>LITTLE RAPUNZEL lets down HER hair but before the HANDSOME PRINCE can climb the tower, ZOMBIES attack and drag HIM off.

RAPUNZEL
Of course, I never noticed a shadowy figure who appeared outside the tower one night.

>LITTLE RICK enters, cloaked.

LITTLE RICK
I'll save you, Little Rapunzel. If it's the last thing I ever do.

>HE exits.

RAPUNZEL
And so, the years passed and I grew up.

>ZOMBIES freeze. LITTLE RAPUNZEL climbs down, and the two RAPUNZELS meet.

RAPUNZEL
You did a great job, Little Me.

LITTLE RAPUNZEL
Thank you, Older Me.

RAPUNZEL
Same time, tomorrow?

LITTLE RAPUNZEL
You bet!

SHE exits. RAPUNZEL climbs the tower.

RAPUNZEL
As I was saying, the years passed…and we ALL grew up.

MOTHER NEGAN enters.

MOTHER NEGAN
Rapunzel! Rapunzel! Let down your long hair!

RAPUNZEL
Do I have to, Mother Negan?

MOTHER NEGAN
Only if you want something to eat, my dear.

RAPUNZEL lets down HER hair.
MOTHER NEGAN attaches a bucket to it.

RAPUNZEL
What's for lunch today? I'm starving.

MOTHER NEGAN
I hope you like Chinese take-out.
(SHE places a take-out bag in the bucket.)

RAPUNZEL
(SHE has pulled up the bucket.)
Hey! Where's my fortune cookie?

MOTHER NEGAN
Don't worry about it. I opened it and your fortune is bad, all bad!
>(She laughs too long and hard at HER own joke.)

RAPUNZEL
Funny. Real funny.

MOTHER NEGAN
I know.

RAPUNZEL
>(To audience.)
If you ever wondered how I used the bathroom for all those years while I was trapped in the tower...
>(SHE lets down the bucket. MOTHER NEGAN hands it to a ZOMBIE who carries it offstage, disgusted.)
Hey, a girl's gotta do what a girl's gotta do.

MOTHER NEGAN
Alright, Rapunzel. Don't you try to escape, I have zombies positioned all around the tower.

RAPUNZEL
Why would I ever try to escape? Just look at this great view.

MOTHER NEGAN
Enjoy it while it lasts. My zombies are spreading out all over the kingdom. Pretty soon I'll rule everything and then you know what I'm going to do?

RAPUNZEL
Burn it all to the ground?

MOTHER NEGAN
Burn it all to the...hey! How did you know I was going to say that?

RAPUNZEL
Because that's what you always say.

MOTHER NEGAN
Oh yeah, I guess I do.

RAPUNZEL
Don't you think this is a bit much? Just because you were rejected by a boy?

MOTHER NEGAN
What do you mean, rejected? He liked me best!

RAPUNZEL
No, he liked me best!

MOTHER NEGAN
I guess we'll never know, since you wouldn't let me tie him up with your magic hair.

RAPUNZEL
I was trying to spare your feelings. That's the truth!

MOTHER NEGAN
You can't handle the truth!

RAPUNZEL
You were my friend!

MOTHER NEGAN
And now I'm your jailer! Ta-ta, Rapunzel, I'm off to the forest with Lucille.

SHE exits.

RAPUNZEL
Lucille was Mother Negan's bat. She took it with her wherever she went. Lucille was her secret weapon...and speaking of secret weapons, my father, the King, had been busy creating a secret weapon of his own.

> The KING enters. Addresses audience.

KING
My poor little daughter has been trapped in that tower for far too long! And now a zombie horde threatens to take over the entire kingdom...but I will not allow it! I have assembled the best zombie fighters in all the land to rescue Rapunzel and defeat Mother Negan and her minions!

RAPUNZEL
That's my Pop!

KING
First, is a giant of a man and one of the meanest zombie fighters around...Abraham Lincoln Mercury Plymouth Isuzu Chrysler Dodge Ford.

> HE enters. A large, severe looking soldier.

RAPUNZEL
Isuzu?

ABRAHAM
(To RAPUNZEL.)

On my mother's side.

(To audience.)

I was a knight, a good one. I have no problem following orders because that's what a good soldier does. It's all about the mission with me, and my mission is to rescue that princess in that tower and to do as much collateral damage to those ugly, good for nothing, brain-eaters as possible. Think of me as a human battering ram, because that is what I am. My name is Abraham Lincoln Mercury Plymouth Isuzu Chrysler Dodge Ford.

RAPUNZEL

Isuzu?

ABRAHAM
(To RAPUNZEL.)

On my mother's side.

KING

Next is my thief, Sneaky Glenn.

> SNEAKY GLENN sneaks in, around and even inside the tower.

SNEAKY GLENN

I'm Sneaky Glenn and I'm probably the best procurer of items in the entire kingdom. You want it? I can get it for you. You need an eight track tape of Red Sovine? I'm your guy. Tickets to the Metropolitan Ballet? I've got them. Pickled pigs feet? More than you could ever eat. An autographed picture of Mary Lou Retton? It'll be yours faster than you can blink.

RAPUNZEL

How about a ladder?

SNEAKY GLENN
(Pause.)
I'll have to get back to you.

KING
Sneaky Glenn's wife, Doctor Maggie.

DOCTOR MAGGIE enters.

DOCTOR MAGGIE
I'm not actually a doctor. My father was a doctor...well, actually he was a veterinarian and I sort of assisted him...sometimes. Really I just watched him operate on cows and pigs and chickens and goats and ducks and helped him bury them when they inevitably died. But here in the dark ages that basically qualifies me as a medical expert. We have this brand new procedure which I've been dying to try out too! It's very cutting edge!

RAPUNZEL
What's it called?

DOCTOR MAGGIE
Amputation.

RAPUNZEL
What's it good for?

DOCTOR MAGGIE
Everything from the common cold to an ingrown toenail.

RAPUNZEL
I'm suddenly feeling extra healthy.

KING
Marlene and Darlene Dixon

THEY enter. MARLENE has an ax hand.
DARLENE carries a crossbow.

MARLENE AND DARLENE
Howdy y'all.

MARLENE
I'm Marlene.

DARLENE
And I'm Darlene.

MARLENE AND DARLENE
And we'se related.

MARLENE
And I is the oldest.

DARLENE
And I is the smartest.

MARLENE
T'aint neither.

DARLENE
Am too.

MARLENE
T'aint.

DARLENE
Am too.

THEY start to fight.

RAPUNZEL
Girls! Quit fighting each other. Save it for the zombies!

MARLENE AND DARLENE
Ok.

RAPUNZEL
Hey Marlene, what happened to your hand?

MARLENE
I ate it.

RAPUNZEL
You ate your own hand?

MARLENE
Yep.

RAPUNZEL
Why'd you do that?

MARLENE
I's hungry.

RAPUNZEL
Makes sense to me. What about you, Darlene? Are you an archer?

DARLENE
What's an archer?

RAPUNZEL
Someone who shoots arrows with a crossbow.

DARLENE
Nope.

RAPUNZEL
Isn't that a crossbow?

DARLENE
Yep.

RAPUNZEL
Then that makes you an archer!

DARLENE
Nope.

RAPUNZEL
Why not?

DARLENE
Ain't got no arrows.

RAPUNZEL
Then what do you do with it?

DARLENE
Stand around and look cool.

> THEY strike a pose.

KING
Granny Carol.

> GRANNY CAROL enters slowly, walking on a cane.

RAPUNZEL
Aren't you a little old to be fighting zombies?

> GRANNY CAROL does a few swings with HER cane and does a cartwheel.

GRANNY CAROL
You were saying?

RAPUNZEL
Holy guacamole! Where'd you learn moves like that?

GRANNY CAROL
I was a cheerleader.

RAPUNZEL
Sign me up!

KING
Michelin the Samurai.

> MICHELIN enters. Takes out HER katana and swings it around.

MICHELIN
I'll do whatever it takes to protect the people I care about.

RAPUNZEL
Your sword is amazing.

MICHELIN
Katana.

RAPUNZEL
Rapunzel.

MICHELIN
Katana.

RAPUNZEL
I beg your pardon?

MICHELIN
It's a katana. A long, curved, single-edged sword traditionally used by Japanese Samurai.

RAPUNZEL
Where'd you get it?

MICHELIN
At a flea market.

RAPUNZEL
Oh?

MICHELIN
Yes. I got a very good deal on it.

RAPUNZEL
So…you aren't a samurai?

MICHELIN
Not originally, no. I was an accountant.

RAPUNZEL
An accountant?

MICHELIN
Indeed.

RAPUNZEL
And now you're a zombie hunting samurai?

MICHELIN
I am…except during tax season.

KING
And their leader, Constable Rick Grimey!

RICK GRIMEY enters.

RAPUNZEL
Rick Grimey? Is that you?

RICK GRIMEY
I promised I'd rescue you, Rapunzel. I've spent my life training for this operation. I worked my way up from dog walker to Constable and helped the King put together this team of zombie fighting specialists. Wait a minute! Where are my kids? Kids? Kids?

JUDITH GRIMEY enters.

JUDITH
Here I am, Papa.

RICK GRIMEY
Who are you?

JUDITH
Judith.

RICK GRIMEY
Judith! Where's your brother?

JUDITH
I don't know. He was right behind me.

RICK GRIMEY
(Yelling.)
CORAL?

EVERYONE
CORAL? CORAL? CORAL?

> CORAL enters. HE wears a hat and a bandage over HIS eye.

CORAL
Here I am!

RICK GRIMEY
Thank goodness! Don't you ever wander off like that boy, do you hear me?

CORAL
Yes, Papa.

JUDITH
What about me?

RICK GRIMEY
What about you?

JUDITH
Aren't you worried about me wandering off?

RICK GRIMEY
Who are you again?

JUDITH
Judith? Your daughter?

> RICK GRIMEY looks at HER confused.

RAPUNZEL
So, Rick…I see you have kids. Is there a Mrs. Grimey?

RICK GRIMEY
That's a long story. Let's just say she got ate by zombies and leave it at that.

RAPUNZEL
So…you're single then?
> (EVERYONE turns and looks at HER.)

Too soon?
> (EVERYONE nods yes.)

Sorry.

RICK GRIMEY
Alright everyone, we're going to attack the zombies guarding the tower and rescue Rapunzel and show off our mad fighting skills in the process.

> MUSIC: EPIC BATTLE MUSIC begins as individually and collectively the ZOMBIE HUNTERS and KING fight the ZOMBIES in an impressive display of stage combat skills. The KING and MARLENE are dragged offstage.

> However, eventually the ZOMBIE
> HUNTERS are over-powered and forced to
> THEIR knees. MOTHER NEGAN enters.

MOTHER NEGAN

Well, well, well. What have we here? If it isn't my old pal, Little Rick Grimey and it looks like Rick has brought along some new friends. Hello, Rick's friends.

ZOMBIE HUNTERS
> (With no enthusiasm.)

Hello.

MOTHER NEGAN

I guess you've come to rescue the Princess?

RICK GRIMEY

Nope. We've come to hunt mushrooms. Isn't that right, fellas?

ZOMBIE HUNTERS

Yes. That's right. I think I see one. I like mushrooms. Etc.

MOTHER NEGAN

Don't play me like I'm some fool. I know why you're here and now I'm going to have to teach you a lesson. I have someone I want you to meet. A very good friend of mine. A very THIRSTY friend of mine. My bat, Lucille.

> MUSIC: Spooky vampire music plays as
> LUCILLE enters. SHE is a cute, little bat.

LUCILLE

How many times do I have to tell you? I am not a vampire bat.

MOTHER NEGAN

Then what kind of bat, are you?

                    LUCILLE
The cute kind.

                    MOTHER NEGAN
See these people, Lucille? I want you to teach them a lesson.

                    LUCILLE
What do you mean? Like a piano lesson?

                    ZOMBIE HUNTERS like this idea.

                    MOTHER NEGAN
No. Not a piano lesson. I mean, a lesson lesson. I want you to give them…the treatment.

                    LUCILLE
All of them?

                    MOTHER NEGAN
Yes, all of them!

                    LUCILLE
But then the play will be over.

                    MOTHER NEGAN
Fine. Pick one.

                    LUCILLE
Eenie. Meanie. Miney. Moe. Catch a tiger by the toe. If he hollers, let him go. My mother told me to pick the very best one and you are not it.

                    SHE points at ABRAHAM. LUCILLE
                    tickles ABRAHAM. HE laughs hysterically
                    until…

                    ABRAHAM
Great oogly moogly!

HE falls forward.

MOTHER NEGAN
I guess he was ticklish.

DARLENE stands up.

DARLENE
That was not cool!

ZOMBIE shoves HER down.

MOTHER NEGAN
You think that wasn't cool? Try this!

SHE points at SNEAKY GLENN.
LUCILLE tickles SNEAKY GLENN. HE
laughs hysterically.

DOCTOR MAGGIE
Sneaky Glenn!

SNEAKY GLENN
Maggie…I think I left the stove on!

HE falls over.

DOCTOR MAGGIE
The stove? Oh no!

DARLENE
Also, not cool!

MOTHER NEGAN
Zombies, take the new recruits off to the make-up lady.
They're ours now. Let this be a lesson to all of you…Mother
Negan knows best!

SHE exits.

RICK GRIMEY
What'll we do now?

RAPUNZEL
I don't know.

JUDITH
I have an idea.

RICK GRIMEY
Who are you again?

EVERYONE
JUDITH!

RICK GRIMEY
Oh! Judith!

RAPUNZEL
What's your idea?

JUDITH
It's an invention more than an idea really.
    (SHE pulls out dynamite.)
I call this dynamite.

RAPUNZEL
What's it do?

JUDITH
It goes boom.

ZOMBIE HUNTERS
I like it! Sounds good! Etc!

JUDITH
We're going to need some rope. Lots of rope.

RAPUNZEL
Where are you going to find rope around here?

EVERYONE looks up at HER.

RICK GRIMEY
Rapunzel, Rapunzel, let down your long hair.

RAPUNZEL
Are you kidding me?

JUDITH
We're also going to need some brains.

RICK GRIMEY
Brains? In this kingdom? Good luck!

GRANNY CAROL
I know a place where we can get all the brains we want.

MICHELIN
Where's that, Granny Carol?

GRANNY CAROL
Brain Hut.

ALL
BRAIN HUT???

GRANNY CAROL
They have an excellent selection of brains all in a nice, relaxed, family-friendly atmosphere.

CORAL
What about kids? Do they have anything for kids?

GRANNY CAROL

Why certainly! Their kid's menu contains numerous items that kids adore like brain nuggets and brain and cheese pizza at very affordable prices, and on Monday nights, kids eat free with the purchase of an adult entrée.

CORAL

That sounds great!

DARLENE

What about peasants? Do they have anything for peasants like me?

GRANNY CAROL

Let me think…they have Mountain Dew.

DARLENE

Woohoo! My favorite!

SHE does a little dance.

RAPUNZEL

Can we get back to the matter at hand? This is starting to sound like a commercial.

RICK GRIMEY

Of course, Rapunzel. Does everyone know what they need to do?

ALL

I do! Yes! You can count on me! Etc!

ALL exit except RICK. RAPUNZEL cuts HAIR with giant scissors and hands it to HIM.

RICK GRIMEY

Don't worry, Rapunzel. We're going to win.

HE exits.

RAPUNZEL

Oh yeah, he liked me best without a doubt.
> (Pause.)

And so they put their plan in place to defeat Mother Negan and her zombie horde, once and for all.

MOTHER NEGAN
> (Enters with ZOMBIES.)

What plan would that be?

RAPUNZEL

Oops. None of your business.

MOTHER NEGAN

Is that so?

RAPUNZEL

That's so.

MOTHER NEGAN

Well, I'm going to make it my business. I'm about to unleash the biggest zombie horde this kingdom has ever seen, and they are going to burn it to the ground! They will be led by its former rulers. Your parents!

> The KING and QUEEN enter, now ZOMBIES.

RAPUNZEL

Mother and Father! NO!!!

KING AND QUEEN

Brains! Brains! Brains!

> ALL ZOMBIES enter.

ALL ZOMBIES
BRAINS! BRAINS! BRAINS!

MICHELIN
(Entering with a bag.)
Did someone say brains?

ZOMBIES cross towards HER.

ZOMBIES
Brains! Brains! Brains!

GRANNY CAROL
(Enters from other side of stage.)
Dinner is served!

SOME ZOMBIES cross to GRANNY
CAROL. CORAL and JUDITH enter.

CORAL AND JUDITH
(Sing-songy. EVERYONE, including ZOMBIES,
join in.)
Brains, brains, the musical fruit. The more you eat, the more you toot! The more you toot, the better you feel, so eat brains with every meal!

MOTHER NEGAN
What do you zombies think you're doing?

RICK GRIMEY enters.

RICK GRIMEY
Now...while they're divided, attack!

MUSIC: Battle Music. There is a large battle. The ZOMBIES are defeated and tied to the tower. The ZOMBIE HUNTERS surround MOTHER NEGAN.

MOTHER NEGAN
You think you've won but you're wrong.
(Yells.)
Oh, Lucille!

LUCILLE enters.

LUCILLE
What is it now?

MOTHER NEGAN
I need you to take care of these Zombie Hunters, once and for all!

LUCILLE
Do I have to?

MOTHER NEGAN
You have to!

LUCILLE
Oh, very well, who gets tickled first?

Suddenly, TIGER enters, and chases LUCILLE and MOTHER NEGAN offstage. THEY scream.

RICK GRIMEY
I certainly didn't see that one coming.

ALL
Me either. Yes. That was surprising. Talk about Deus Ex Machina. Etc.

RICK GRIMEY
We've defeated the zombie horde, but Rapunzel is still trapped in the tower.

RAPUNZEL
Trapped?
>(SHE enters from behind the tower.)

I was never trapped. Not really.

ALL
RAPUNZEL!!!

RICK GRIMEY
How'd you escape the tower?

RAPUNZEL
The same way I got in. I used the back door.

ALL
BACK DOOR???

MICHELIN
You mean, there was a back door this whole time?

RAPUNZEL
Yes.

DARLENE
Then why didn't you use it to escape?

RAPUNZEL
The place was always surrounded by zombies! And besides, where's the drama in that?

ALL
I guess she's right. Yes. I love drama. That is why we're here. Etc.

GRANNY CAROL
Speaking of zombies, what are we supposed to do with them?

JUDITH
That's where my dynamite comes in.

SHE places it behind the tower.

CORAL

What happens now?

JUDITH

It goes boom.

ALL

BOOM???

SOUND: BOOM! ZOMBIE HUNTERS cower on the edges of stage. The tower launches like a rocket offstage. LIGHTS: Flash and smoke. Body parts lay around. ALL return to center, rubbing THEIR ears. All lines until the end of the play are shouted because of the hearing damage caused by the blast.

RICK GRIMEY

Wonder where'll they land?

RAPUNZEL

I'm sure they'll turn up in another fairy tale kingdom somewhere.

RICK GRIMEY

I'm sorry about your parents, Rapunzel. They were a good king and queen.

GRANNY CAROL

I guess this makes you the new queen.

RAPUNZEL

I suppose so.
(SHE looks at RICK.)
Would you like to be my king?

RICK GRIMEY

Me?

RAPUNZEL

The job is yours, if you want it.
    (SHE wraps HER hair around HIM.)
What do you say, Rick Grimey? After all this time, who did you like better...me or Negan?

RICK GRIMEY

Well...

RAPUNZEL

Rick?

RICK GRIMEY
NEGAN! OK! I LIKED NEGAN BETTER!

ALL
SAY WHAT???

RAPUNZEL
You liked Negan better than me?

RICK GRIMEY
What can I say? I don't care for blondes.

    MOTHER NEGAN enters.

MOTHER NEGAN

Told you so!

    MOTHER NEGAN and RAPUNZEL have
    a knockdown, drag out fight, the likes of
    which have never been seen before. EPIC
    BATTLE MUSIC plays until both of THEM
    are winded, and barely standing.

MOTHER NEGAN
(Breathing hard.)
I told you he liked me best.

RAPUNZEL

Touché.
(Holds out HER hand.)
Friends?

MOTHER NEGAN
(Shakes hands with RAPUNZEL.)
Friends.

EVERYONE cheers.

RAPUNZEL
And they all lived happily ever after…or did they?
(SHE holds up HER arm with a bite taken out.)

ALL gasp. LIGHTS: Blackout.

THE END

Thank you for purchasing and reading this play. If you enjoyed it, we'd appreciate a review on Amazon.com.

On the following pages you will find a selection of other plays from the Black Box Theatre Publishing Company catalog presented for you at no additional cost.

Enjoy!!!

www.blackboxtheatrepublishing.com

NOW AVAILABLE!!!

"Poop Happens!" in this family friendly cowboy comedy!

So, Who Was That Masked Guy Anyway? is the story of Ernie, the grandson of the original Masked Cowboy, a lawman who fought for truth, justice and the cowboy way in the old west. Now that Grandpa is getting on in years he's looking for someone to carry on for him. The only problem? Ernie doesn't know anything about being a cowboy. He's never seen a real cow, he's allergic to milk and to tell the truth he doesn't know one end of a horse from another...but beware, before it's all over, the poop is sure to hit the fans!

Cast Size: 21 Flexible M-F Roles Doubling Possible.

Royalties: $50.00 per performance.

Running Time: Approximately 90 minutes.

NOW AVAILABLE!!!

WANTED: SANTA CLAUS is the story of what happens when a group of department store moguls decide to replace Santa Claus with the shiny new "KRINGLE 3000", codenamed...ROBO-SANTA! Now it's up to Santa's elves to save the day! But Santa's in no shape to take on his stainless steel counterpart! He'll have to train for his big comeback. Enter Mickey, one of the toughest elves of all time! He'll get Santa ready for the big showdown! But it's going to mean reaching deep down inside to find "the eye of the reindeer"!

Cast Size 23 Flexible M-F Roles Doubling Possible.

Royalties: $50.00 per performance.

Running Time: Approximately 90 Minutes.

NOW AVAILABLE!!!

At the edge of the universe sits The Long John Cafe. A place where the average guy and the average "Super" guy can sit and have a cup of coffee and just be themselves...or, someone else if that's what they want. The cafe is populated by iconic figures of the 20th Century, including cowboys, hippies, super heroes and movie stars. They've come to celebrate the end of the old Century and the beginning of tomorrow! That is, if they make it through the night! It seems the evil Dr. McNastiman has other plans for our heroes. Like their total destruction!

Cast Size: 17 9M 8F.

Royalties: $50.00 per performance.

Running Time: Approximately 90 Minutes.

NOW AVAILABLE!!!

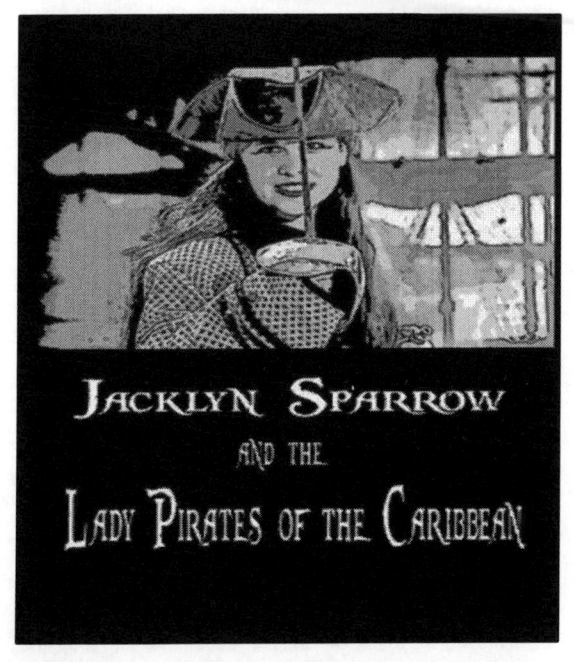

JACKLYN SPARROW
AND THE
LADY PIRATES OF THE CARIBBEAN

Jacklyn Sparrow and the Lady Pirates of the Caribbean is our brand new swashbuckling pirate parody complete with bloodthirsty buccaneers in massive sword clanking battle scenes!! A giant wise cracking parrot named Polly!! Crazy obsessions with eye liner!! And just who is Robert, the Dreaded Phylum Porifera!!!

Please Note: We offer large and small cast versions of this play. Cast and royalty numbers for both are below.

Cast Size: 45/13 Flexible M-F Roles Doubling Possible.

Royalties: $50.00 per performance.

Running Time: Approximately 120/45 Minutes.

NOW AVAILABLE!!!

"May the Dwarf be with you in this wacky take on the classic fairy tale which will have audiences rolling in the floor with laughter!

What happens when you mix an articulate mirror, a conceited queen, a prince dressed in purple, seven little people with personality issues, a basket of kumquats and a little Star Wars for good measure?

Cast Size: 12 Flexible M-F Roles.

Royalty: $50.00 per performance.

Running Time: Approximately 45 Minutes.

NOW AVAILABLE!!!

Dear John
An ode to the potty.

"My dreams of thee flow softly.
They enter with tender rush.
The still soft sound which echoes,
When I lower the lid and flush."

They say that porcelain is the best antenna for creativity. At least that's what this cast of young people believe in Dear John: An ode to the potty! The action of this one act play takes place almost entirely behind the doors of five bathroom stalls. This short comedy is dedicated to all those term papers, funny pages and Charles Dickens' novels that have been read behind closed (stall) doors!

Cast Size: 10 5M 5F.

Royalties: $35.00 per performance.

Running Time: Approximately 15 Minutes.

NOW AVAILABLE!!!

ELVIS MEETS NIXON
(OPERATION WIGGLE)

Declassified after 40 years!

On December 21, 1970, an impromptu meeting took place between the King of Rock and Roll and the Leader of the Free World.

Elvis Meets Nixon (Operation Wiggle) is a short comedy which offers one possible (and ultimately ridiculous) explanation of what happened during that meeting.

Cast Size: 2 M with 1 Offstage F Voice.

Royalties: $35.00 per performance.

Running Time: Approximately 10 Minutes.

NOW AVAILABLE!!!

Even Adam

In the beginning, there was a man.
Then there was a woman.
And then there was this piece of fruit...
...and that's when everything went horribly wrong!
Even Adam is a short comedy exploring the relationship
between men and women right from day one.

Why doesn't he ever bring her flowers like he used to?
Why doesn't she laugh at his jokes anymore?
And just who is that guy in the red suit?
And how did she convince him to eat that fruit, anyway?

Cast Size: 3 2M-1F.

Royalties: $35.00 per performance.

Running Time: Approximately 10 Minutes.

NOW AVAILABLE!!!

THE DRACULA SPECTACULA

Count Dracula is bored. He's pretty much sucked Transylvania dry, and he's looking for a new challenge. So it's off to New York, New York! The Big Apple! The town that never sleeps...that'll pose a challenge for sure. Dracula purchases The Carfax Theatre and decides to put on a big, flashy Broadway show!

Cast Size: 50 Flexible M/F roles with Doubling Possible.

Royalties: $50.00 per performance.

Running Time: Approximately 90 Minutes.

NOW AVAILABLE!!!

THE FOUR PRESIDENTS is an educational play which examines the lives and characters of four of the most colorful personalities to hold the office. George Washington, Abraham Lincoln, Theodore Roosevelt and Richard Nixon. Much of the dialogue comes from the Presidents' own words.

A perfect show for schools!

Cast Size: 10 Flexible M-F Roles with Doubling Possible.

Royalties: $50.00 per performance.

Running Time: Approximately 60 Minutes.

NOW AVAILABLE!!!

The lights rise on a beautiful sunset.
A mermaid is silhouetted against an ocean backdrop.
Hauntingly familiar music fills the air.
Then...the Lawyer shows up.
And that's when the fun really begins!

It's The Little Mermaid (More or Less.)

Cast Size: 30 Flexible M-F Roles with Doubling Possible.

Royalties: $50.00 per performance.

Running Time: Approximately 45 Minutes.

NOW AVAILABLE!!!

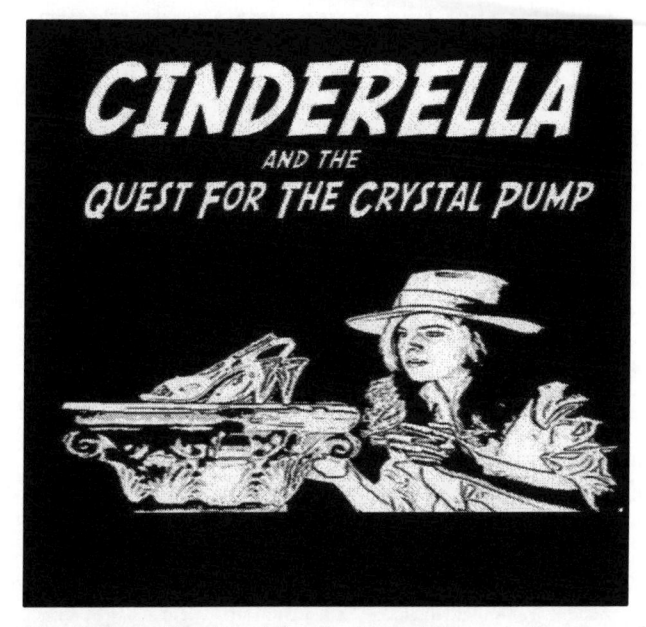

CINDERELLA
AND THE QUEST FOR THE CRYSTAL PUMP

Cinderella and the Quest for the Crystal Pump, is the story of a young girl seeking a life beyond the endless chores heaped upon her by her grouchy stepmother and two stepsisters. But more than anything, Cinderella wants to go to the prince's masquerade ball, but there's one problem...she has nothing to wear! Luckily, her Fairy Godperson has a few ideas.

Please Note: This play is available in large and small cast versions. Both cast sizes and royalty rates are listed below.

Cast Size: 30/13 Flexible M-F Roles with Some Doubling Possible.

Royalties: $50.00 per performance.

Running Time: Approximately 90/45 Minutes.

NOW AVAILABLE!!!

Shorespeare is loosely based on a Midsummer Night's Dream. Shakespeare, with the help of Cupid, has landed at the Jersey Shore. Cupid inspires him to write a play about two New Jersey sweethearts, Cleo and Toni. Shakespeare is put off by their accent and way of talking, but decides to send the two teenagers on a course of true love. Toni and Cleo are determined to get married right after they graduate from high school, but in order to do so they must pass this course of true love that Cupid's pixies create and manipulate. As they travel along the boardwalk at the Jersey Shore, Cleo and Toni, meet a handful of historical figures disguised as the carnies. Confucius teaches Cleo the "Zen of Snoring". Charles Ponzi teaches them the importance of "White Lies", Leonardo Da Vinci shows them the "Art of Multitasking", and finally they meet Napolean who tries to help them to "Accept Shortcomings" of each other. After going through all these lessons, the sweethearts decide that marriage should wait, and Cupid is proud of Shakespeare who has finally reached out to the modern youth.

NOW AVAILABLE!!!

Everyone has heard the phrase, "it's the squeaky wheel that gets the oil," but how many people know the Back-story? The story begins in a kingdom far, far away over the rainbow – a kingdom called Spokend. This kingdom of wheels is a happy one for the gods have blessed the tiny hamlet with plentiful sunshine, water and most important –oil. Until a terrible drought starts to dry up all the oil supplies. What is to be done?

The powerful barons of industry and politicians decide to hold a meeting to decide how to solve the situation. Since Spokend is a democracy all the citizens come to the meeting but their voices are ignored – especially the voice of one of the poorer citizens of the community suffering from a squeak that can only be cured with oil, Spare Wheel and his wife Fifth Wheel. Despite Spare Wheel's desperate pleas for oil, he is ignored and sent home without any help or consideration.

Without oil, Spare Wheel's squeak becomes so bad he loses his job and his family starts to suffer when his sick leave and unemployment benefits run out. What is he to do? Spare Wheel and Fifth Wheel develop a scheme that uses the squeak to their advantage against the town magistrate Big Wheel who finally relents and gives over the oil. Thus, for years after in the town of Spokend citizens in need of help are told "It's the squeaky wheel that gets the oil."

NOW AVAILABLE!!!

Once upon a time, a beautiful princess was placed under a magic spell by an evil fairy. A spell that would cause her to fall into a deep, deep sleep. A sleep from which she would awaken 1000 years later.

It's "Sleeping Beauty meets Buck Rogers" in this play for young audiences.

Royalties: $50.00 per performance.

Cast Size: 13 with flexible extras.

Running Time: Approximately 45 minutes.

NOW AVAILABLE!!!

Santa Claus. Frosty. Rudolph. Jack Frost.

This Christmas…if you've got a problem and if you can find them then maybe you can hire…THE SLEIGH TEAM!!!

The team is hired by lowly clerk, Bob Crachit to help his boss, the miserly old Ebenezer Scrooge find a little "Christmas Spirit"!

Royalties: $50.00 per performance.

Cast Size: 6

Running Time: Approximately 45 minutes.

NOW AVAILABLE!!!

The Odd Princesses

The Odd Princesses is a parody/mash-up that opens with a group of princesses assembled for a card game in the palace of the notoriously messy Snow White. Late to arrive to the party is the perpetually neat Cinderella who has run away from home after becoming fed up with being treated like a maid by her stepmother. With no where else to turn, the two total opposites decide to move in together! What could go wrong?

Royalties: $50.00 per performance.

Cast Size: 8 with extras possible.

Running Time: Approximately 45 minutes.

NOW AVAILABLE!!!

Eager to escape the clutches of the Big Bad Wolf once and for all, the Three Little Pigs build a time machine and travel back in time 150 million years to the Jurassic era where they quickly discover they have problems much bigger than the Big Bad Wolf. Much, much, much bigger!!!

Royalties $35.00 per performance.

Cast Size: 6+ extras with flexible M-F roles.

Running Time: Approximately 30 minutes.

NOW AVAILABLE!!!

Dr. Victor "Vickie" Frankenstein has just inherited his grandfather's castle in foggy Transylvania...but what secrets lie in the ultra-secret, sub-terrainian laboratory located beneath the castle??? It's a little bit monster story and a little bit Rock and Roll!

Royalties $50.00 per performance.

Cast Size: 16. 8 principle roles, 8+ Extras possible.

Running Time: Approximately one hour.